SEEKING PEACE

KINGS OF RETRIBUTION MC MONTANA

SANDY ALVAREZ

CRYSTAL DANIELS

TWO PENS-

CRYSTAL *Daniels*

Sandy ALVAREZ

-ONE STORY

1

BLAKE

It's early morning as I move soundlessly through the clubhouse, doing a walkthrough and checking security cameras before stopping outside Grey's bedroom and rapping my knuckles against the door. I wait for a beat until I hear his fist thump against the wall. It's a system of communication we've utilized over the past few years when I'm leaving the compound without making him drag his ass out of bed.

I stroll down the hall, but before leaving the clubhouse, I detour toward Ember's room. Only a couple of hours ago, I left her room after waking up from a dream I couldn't shake off.

I quietly crack open the door, peering inside. The sound of the oscillating fan fills the room, and the breeze it's creating causes the sheer curtains covering the window beside her bed to sway and the brown-tinged gray moonlight to ripple like waves on the surface of the bedroom wall. My eyes land on Ember's sleeping form, lying partially on her stomach with one leg exposed from beneath the covers, revealing the trail of flowers tattooed down her outer thigh.

I'm pathetic.

"Blake?"

Shit. I close my eyes, kicking myself for checking on her in the first place.

"Everything okay?" Her feathery voice fills the room with concern.

Is everything okay? Now there's a loaded question.

"Everything is fine. Making rounds and checking on everyone before heading out."

Ember throws her covers to the side, slides out of bed, and heads in my direction, her bare feet shuffling across the floor. She's wearing white panties and a cropped tee shirt featuring a T-Rex with the word *Rawr* pulled taut across her tits. She pulls the door open a bit more and peers up at me.

"Couldn't sleep?" She yawns, and I feel terrible that I disturbed her.

I can't help but continue to take her in. How can one woman be this goddamn beautiful? Ember's hypnotic gray eyes stare into mine as she waits for me to respond. Strands of hair stick to her long thick lashes as she blinks. I want to reach out and brush the loose locks of hair from her face but restrain myself.

My heart starts thumping against my ribcage. If she only knew what being near her does to my insides.

"Yeah," I answer. The truth is, sleep never comes easy for me and hasn't for years. The only time I find any peace is when Ember plays her music. "I better get goin'."

Ember leans her shoulder against the door frame, not once taking her attention off my face. "Want some coffee before you go?"

Fuck, I love how thoughtful she always is. "No, babe."

A jolt of electricity travels across my skin when she touches my forearm. "I worry about you, Blake. You haven't been sleeping much lately—less than usual. Why don't you come..."

"Go back to bed." I cut her off, knowing what she's about to say. I swallow the feelings her touch ignites and step back, putting space between us while her hand falls from my arm. We've been playing this game for a long time. Much longer than I care to acknowledge. The tension between us is a ticking time bomb waiting to explode, and it's becoming this force of nature that I fight harder against with each passing day.

My mouth goes dry as the thoughts inside my head try like hell to force their way past my lips while Ember looks up at me. She knows I'm fighting myself but says nothing more. Instead, she casts her eyes to the floor and closes her door.

I press my palm to the door, planting my feet, fighting the overwhelming urge to be on the other side. *You can't go there.*

Ultimately, ignoring every cell in my body telling me to crawl back in bed beside Ember, I walk away.

Sometime later, I wipe sweat from my brow, stepping back from the project I've been working on for the past week and scrutinizing every detail carved into the red oak. The client from Alaska commissioned a life-sized replica of a Yukon wolf. Satisfied with my progress, I place the carving tools on the workstation.

A gust of wind blows through the barn, stirring the sawdust and various sizes of wood chips across the dirt floor. Walking to the small cooler on the ground near the barn's opening, I flip back the lid, pluck out a cold bottle of water, and down half while strolling outside.

I sit on the stump of a large tree I had to cut down a couple of weeks ago. Heavy gray clouds hang low in the distance, blotting out the just-risen sun, and the soft rosy hues it casts across the sky muddle into more somber shades. I can see from the top of this hill for miles, overlooking the treetops to a lake in the distance.

Aside from the trees, all that stands on the property is the old barn behind me. I used the money from selling sculptures to purchase my little slice of heaven, and as soon as I save enough, I'll also build a home here.

I lift the filtered end of a cigarette to my lips, light it, and pull in a lungful of nicotine. I hold my breath until my chest burns before exhaling. Considering where I started, I'm a lucky motherfucker to be where I am today. If it weren't for Jake and the others coming into my life when they did, I would probably be dead.

The club means everything to me. I have brothers who would lay down their lives for me. And I would do the same for them. Being a member of Kings of Retribution gives me the purpose and strength to fight. My commitment to the club and my brothers goes beyond loyalty, because they gave a damn about my life when I couldn't. They are my family.

I was chasing death at one point in my past. Existing felt like this massive weight bearing down on me. I was suffocating. Addiction slowly sucked the soul out of me. For a long time, I was a dead man walking. Honestly, I preferred it that way, because feeling anything other than nothing was better than reality and the pain I was hiding. That's the way addiction works. It feeds off all the insecurities, negative energy, and trauma a body is holding on to and tricks a person into thinking they can't live without it. The addiction gives a false sense of security, but no matter how good it feels during the high, that warm embrace is a lie.

I take a cleansing breath. My demons don't have their claws sunk into my skin, but I'm acutely aware of their ever-looming presence lurking in the shadows, waiting for the right moment of weakness to present itself. Every day I wake up and choose life. Some days are harder than others, but when I look at the people in my life, I dust myself off and keep moving forward.

. . .

Several hours later, I'm at my day job, finishing up a floral sternum tattoo for a chic named Stacy, a client of mine. "You got plans tonight?" she asks.

I keep my head down, focused and the task at hand. "Why?"

"I thought maybe you could come over to my place?" she says, hopeful. I lift the needle from her skin, place it on the table beside me, and glance at her but say nothing. "Don't you miss me?" she pouts.

Choosing not to hurt her feelings, I stay silent. Her clinginess is why I haven't fucked her in some time. "You could invite me back to the clubhouse."

I quickly squash her hopes. "Not happenin'." I grab some clean paper towels and the bottle of green soap nearby and clean the tattoo. "Take a look," I tell her, cleaning my station.

Stacy slides from the table and stands in front of the mirror. "It's beautiful, Blake." Then she turns to face me so I can cover the fresh ink with an adhesive bandage. "Come on. Didn't I mean more to you than just sex?" she whines, continuing in her attempt to lure me. Stacy closes the gap between us. From the corner of my eye, I notice Gabriel shaking his head, clearly overhearing my current situation. "I can't stop thinking about you."

"We haven't fucked in over a year. Move on." I show no interest in her campaign to get me in her bed again.

"I haven't seen you with anyone else in town." She falls silent, and for a second, I think she's about to give up, but she continues through laughter, "Are you fucking a club whore?"

I cut my eyes at her, anger twisting my gut. "Just because I fucked that cunt of yours doesn't give you claim over me, and it sure as shit doesn't give you leeway to question whom I choose to have in my bed."

Stacy's face reddens with anger and humiliation because I wasn't subtle or quiet with my words.

"You know what? Fuck you, Blake. I'm better than any whore."

Her words anger me further, but I stay seated. She snatches her bag from the floor, digs around inside, tosses some tip money at my feet then stomps out of the shop.

I continue cleaning up and sanitizing my equipment.

"That escalated quickly. She's batshit crazy." Grey watches Stacy out the shop window as she climbs into her car. "Told you she was trouble," he pipes up.

"I don't need the *I told you so's*." I run my palm over my face.

"Fine. How about a beer, and I kick your ass in a game of pool?" Grey twirls his keys around his finger, eager to hit the road back to the clubhouse.

Thankful for the change of subject matter, I nod. "Alright, and to sweeten the deal, the loser washes all the club members' bikes this weekend," I wager, my mood shifting for the better.

"I'll do you one better. The loser washes the bikes while wearing a pair of daisy dukes." Grey grins.

I let out a hearty laugh. "You're goin' down, brother."

Grey looks past me at Gabriel, who has gotten up. "Anything else I should grab from Charley's, besides those few cases of whiskey, on the way home?"

"Grab the women a few bottles of that fruity shit they like mixing drinks with," Gabriel grumbles in his usual manner.

"You got it!" Grey shouts over his shoulder as he steps out the door.

Before I take my leave, Gabriel stops me by saying, "It's easier when you stop runnin'."

"Runnin' from what?" I'm curious about where this conversation is going, seeing that Gabriel isn't much of a conversationalist.

"Not what—who."

He doesn't have to elaborate. I know to whom he is referring. Hell, every club member has witnessed the dance Ember and I have been performing for a couple of years. "She deserves better."

"Don't you think she should get to decide that for herself?" Gabriel hits me with another gut punch of reality, and I have no rebuttal.

Later in the night, everyone is gathered at the clubhouse, enjoying drinks and good music. After beating Grey at three games of pool, I toss the cue stick onto the table, wearing an ear-to-ear smile, knowing I won't be sudsing up chrome with my ass hanging out.

Quinn strolls across the room to where he craftily displayed a pair of cutoff jeans by pinning them to the corkscrew board near the front door with two small pocket knives. "How about a pregame show before the main event?" Quinn teases as he tosses the shorts at Grey, then sits beside Gabriel and pulls Emerson back on his lap.

"Fuck, man. You didn't have to cut them so damn short." Grey holds the denim to his waist. "How the hell am I supposed to keep my dick contained?" He inspects the narrow strip of denim holding the crotch of the shorts together.

"A thong will keep your frank and beans tucked away and still keep your cheeks freely exposed in the back," Quinn says casually, and all eyes fall on him. "What?" He glances around the room. "They make them for guys and they are no different from a jockstrap." He shrugs, downing his drink.

"Jesus," Gabriel grumbles, and Alba giggles beside him. Across the table, Sam can't control his laughter and Sofia is blushing.

"Hey, big guy, don't knock it till you try it. How about I buy you a pair?" Quinn can't help but poke the bear.

"How bout I shove my size thirteen foot up your ass," Gabriel growls.

Before Quinn can continue to goad Gabriel further, Alba turns and whispers something in her man's ear. Gabriel quickly gets to his feet, holding tight to his woman. "Takin' my woman home."

The room fills with laughter.

Alba waves goodbye as she and Gabriel retreat, heading home.

"We're done for the night, too." Sam stands, and Sofia joins him. "We'll catch y'all tomorrow."

A couple of hours later, everyone else is on their way home, while those of us remaining clean the place up before locking it down and heading to bed.

After a quick shower, I lie in bed for the longest time, staring out the window and watching another storm roll in. Lightning illuminates the night, followed by thunder rattling the windowpane.

Ember playing the cello echoes through the clubhouse. Like a moth to a flame, I climb out of bed, drawn to her. I follow the music, stopping outside her door. Like a hundred times before, I try to talk myself out of going inside. The battle lost, I slowly turn the handle and walk inside, looking for my next fix. Ember's eyes stay closed as she runs the bow over the strings, but her lips lift in a smile when they open and connect with mine.

I'm addicted, and my drug of choice is her.

2

EMBER

It's the same song and dance between Blake and me every night. The sad part is I allow it to keep happening, even though I wake up to an empty bed each morning. And each morning, the loss of his presence causes another piece of my heart to shatter. The really fucked up part about all this is I will continue allowing him in my bed and my heart, because I'm in love with him. I'm in love with a man who isn't capable of loving me back. I see it in his eyes each time he looks at me. His unhappiness imprisons him. Blake's past has a chokehold on his future, as if the Devil himself has a fist around his neck. I don't know the entirety of Blake's story, but the bits and pieces that have slipped over the past couple of years are enough for me to understand why he is the way he is. And what makes our relationship work is that I accept the small pieces of himself he shares, and I don't demand more than he's capable of giving.

Regarding Blake's and my relationship, there are no expectations or rules. He is who he is, and I am who I am. I know what everyone else thinks when it comes to Blake and me. I see the sly looks from the women and knowing grins from the men.

There have even been playful comments about Blake sneaking in and out of my room at night. Nevertheless, he never bothers correcting them, and neither do I. I'd like to think what Blake and I have is unique.

With the moonlight casting a glow on the bed where Blake lies, head propped up on my pillow, hands resting on his stomach, and eyes on me, I play "Yesterday" by The Beatles. My body is hyper-aware of his gaze as each note dances off my fingertips. Some nights he falls asleep in minutes, and others, he will watch me for hours. I don't dare stop playing until his body gives up the fight. Whether I play for ten minutes or two hours, I only notice him at peace.

Reaching the last note, I take a deep breath and slowly open my eyes. A calmness blankets the room, and I notice Blake sleeping peacefully. I sit a moment and take in all that he is. Blake's large, six-foot-two body looks enormous in my queen-sized bed. His dark brown hair is cropped close on the sides but is longer on top. Most of the time, it's a mess, like he's constantly running his hand through it. Blake doesn't grow a beard like most of the guys in the club. Instead, he often has a few days-worth of stubble.

Standing, I set my cello in its stand and pad over to my side of the bed. Lifting the sheet, I settle in beside him. With my cheek resting on the palm of my hand, I study his face like I do every night and gently brush back the lock of dark hair that has fallen over his forehead. This is where Blake and I differ. While he chases sleep, I fight it. Because I know that come morning, he will be gone.

The following day, I know I'm alone before opening my eyes. I ignore the ache in my chest as I roll over and look at the time. It's nearly dawn, and the sun is starting to peek through the curtains. I reach across the bed and touch the spot where Blake slept to find the sheets still warm. Though the bed is warm, losing his presence chills me.

Not wanting to put a damper on my day, I push thoughts of Blake aside and climb out of bed. Today is Sunday, which means everyone will be rolling in shortly. No matter how busy life gets, Sundays are reserved for family brunch. That means I need to get a move on and help Lisa in the kitchen.

"Morning, Ember." Lisa greets me with pep as she whips up pancake batter.

"Morning." I smile.

"I just brewed a fresh pot of coffee. Why don't you grab a cup?"

"You're the best." I kiss her cheek. "I'll start the eggs and sausage."

"Thanks, doll."

While I gulp down my coffee, I get started on the eggs. "Where's Raine?" I ask.

Lisa glances back over her shoulder. "We were running low on bread and juice, so she went on a store run."

"Is that cinnamon I smell?" Quinn comes barging into the kitchen, rubbing his stomach. Emerson and their little girl Lydia are trailing behind him. Emerson rolls her eyes. "Quinn, you ate three donuts on the way over and half of Lydia's banana that fell on the car floor." Emerson scrunches her face.

"What?" Quinn looks offended. "I wasn't about to let food go to waste."

Emerson blinks. "It had hair and stale cereal stuck to it."

Quinn just grins and shrugs his shoulders while his daughter giggles. Emerson shakes her head and looks at me. "I married that."

I burst out laughing. "That you did."

. . .

"What's everyone laughing about?" Alba walks into the kitchen with her daughter on her hip. Behind her is Gabriel and his mini-me, little Gabe.

"What stupid shit has Quinn done now?" Gabriel slaps Quinn on the back.

"Hey, why do you assume I've done something stupid?" Quinn grumbles. Gabriel gives Quinn a blank look, making everyone laugh harder.

"You know what. I'm not feelin' the love, so I'm just going to take my cinnamon roll—" he reaches past Lisa and snatches a roll from the tray "—and go see what Prez is up to." Quinn makes his dramatic exit, and Gabriel follows behind, shaking his head.

"Is there anything you need help with?" Alba asks.

I shake my head. "I think we have it covered." I smile and turn toward Lydia. "But I could use some help whisking these eggs."

"Me! Me! Me! I can help." Lydia cheers. "I'm a good whisker. I help Mommy all the time."

"Perfect. You can help me then." I pull a stool toward the counter and grab one of Lisa's aprons from the refrigerator hook. "Let's wear this, so we don't mess up your pretty dress." Lydia steps up on the stool, and I help her with the apron. "How are you at cracking eggs?" I ask.

She claps her hands. "I'm good at that part, and Daddy says I hardly get any shells in the bowl."

"Well, Miss Lydia, let's get to crackin' and whiskin' then. I'd hate for your daddy to go hungry."

Lydia scrunches her nose, giving me a serious look. "But Daddy is always hungry."

Later that morning, as I sit at the table, I realize I live for these moments with the people I consider my family. No matter the ups and downs the club goes through or the challenges we face, this makes life worth living.

At eighteen, I started dating this guy who was twenty-one. We had run in the same circle since we were kids, and our parents had been friends for as long as I could remember. I wasn't crazy about Devan, but I tolerated him. He came along during my rebellious stage. I started rebelling not long after my seventeenth birthday. By the time I turned eighteen, I'd been picked up three times by the police for public intoxication and arrested once during a raid at a house party. My father, of course, got me out of trouble each time. His people were always good at sweeping things under the rug, because God forbid the public got wind of my indiscretions. It wasn't even about me; it was about my parents' reputations. And not once did my mom and dad stop to ask themselves or me why I was acting out.

I just wanted to be seen. I wanted them to care. But pretty soon, I stopped caring. That's where Devan came in. He had no problem providing alcohol when I wanted it, and he knew guys who could hook us up when we were looking to get high. For two years, I spiraled. All I cared about was partying and being with friends. My parents stayed on my ass and demanded I do something with the education I'd worked so hard for; to make something of myself. But that wasn't what I wanted. I didn't want their life; I wanted my own.

The event that would forever alter my path in life came the summer after I turned twenty.

One day, Devan decides we'll go to Vegas. I get a bad feeling in my gut when he suggests it, because Devan has recently developed a gambling problem. It's how he makes money to score drugs. They aren't small sums of money, either.

Recently, Devan got into serious trouble with a loan shark when he couldn't pay back the twenty thousand dollars he'd lost playing cards. His parents bailed him out, making him promise no more gambling. That lasted about a week.

Now, despite my bad feelings, I go with him. On day two of the drive from Georgia to Vegas, we stop at some hole-in-the-wall biker bar in New Mexico. I know Devan and I don't belong as soon as we enter the bar. I beg him to leave, and he promises we will after one drink. For Devan, one drink turns into five. I start panicking when he weasels into a card game some bikers are having at the back of the bar. Two hours later, Devan has lost all his cash, as well as my watch, necklace, and the diamond earrings I got from my grandmother before she passed away. And instead of cutting his losses, Devan continues playing, even though he has nothing left to give. When it's all said and done, Devan has lost the last game and owes a biker named Rip two thousand dollars neither of us has.

"Come on, man, I don't have the two grand, but I'm good for it." Devan gurgles "please" as Rip presses his forearm harder against his throat.

"Please let him go!" I struggle against the hold Rip's biker friend has on me. "He'll pay you the money. He just needs a little time."

"Shut up, bitch," Rip sneers. Then he turns back to Devan. "Saw you drive up in a fancy-ass car."

I watch as Devan's eyes go big. He loves that car, and the brand-new black BMW is just as pretentious as him. "Not the car, man. Anything but my car."

A sinister grin spreads across Rip's face as though those were the words he wanted to hear. He removes his arm from Devan's throat and says, "Either I take the car, or I take the girl."

Suddenly there is a ringing in my ears, and I break out in a cold sweat. "Wh—what?" I look at Devan. "Give him the keys, Devan." Except Devan isn't looking at me. He's looking at the man like he's actually contemplating the deal. "Devan, give him the keys." I kick and struggle when I don't see Devan coming to my defense. "Seriously,

Devan! Give him the keys." Finally, Devan looks at me. He seems almost apologetic...almost.

"I'm sorry." He turns back to the big biker. "You can have her."

"Devan!" I cry after him while trying to fight off the hold on me. "Devan, don't leave me here! Come back!"

Suddenly, out of nowhere, all hell breaks loose when a man I hadn't noticed before breaks a bar stool over the top of Rip's head, causing him to drop like a sack of potatoes. The next thing I know, his friend's bruising grip on me is gone. Stumbling over my feet, I turn to find a man with a bushy beard holding a gun to the jerk's head. I notice his leather vest with a patch on the chest that reads President. There's another man behind him with the same vest. Only his patch reads Doc.

"This is what's going to happen. I'm walkin' out of this shit hole with that girl. Any of you motherfuckers get a wild hair and try following us, I won't hesitate puttin' a bullet in your head." The man looks at me, and even though he's holding a gun, the gentleness in his blue eyes tells me I can trust him. "Let's go, darlin'."

Nodding, I stick close to his side and follow his lead out of the bar and to his motorcycle. "Here." He hands me a helmet. "Hurry up and climb on."

"Prez," his friend says. "We ain't got no backup. We need to get the fuck out of here and fast."

Seconds later, we're peeling out of the parking lot.

"You good over there, darlin'?" A deep voice brings me back to the present.

I look over at Jake, who is watching me intently, and I smile. "I'm good."

3

BLAKE

My eyes land on my father's and another club member's bikes parked in the driveway when I step off the school bus, and my stomach knots up with anxiety. I find my dad sitting on the sofa, leaning over the coffee table, snorting white powder up his nose. He raises his head and glares at me with disdain. "Get me a fuckin' beer," he grunts, tilting his head back and pinching his nose. At nine years old, seeing someone snort cocaine is normal for me. How fucked up is that?

"Where's my mom?"

"None of your goddamn business. Get that damn beer before I snatch a knot in your head," my father sneers.

As I head for the refrigerator, Maddog, the club's enforcer, steps out of my mom's room, zipping up his pants. His cold stare lands on me, and he smirks. I rush past him to find my mom sobbing at the foot of the bed.

"Mom." My voice cracks. She lifts her head, revealing a swollen, busted lip and welts on her cheek, and her eyes fill with fresh tears. I struggle to contain the rage building up in my body, until something inside me snaps. I walk over to the nightstand, where I've seen a handgun before, and open the drawer. I know jack shit about guns, but I wrap my hand around the handle.

"Blake, no!" Mom cries, but I leave the bedroom before she can stop me.

Maddog and my father are in the living room, huddled around the coffee table and counting out stacks of money. Maddog sees me raise the weapon in my hand first and goes for his gun, which grabs my father's attention. I point the gun at my father and pull the trigger.

Laughter fills the room as my father flies off the couch and has the tip of his gun pressed against my forehead. "You should have checked it for bullets first." My heart is pounding out of my chest, but I stand tall, trying not to show fear.

"No, please." My mom enters the room, pleading for my father to put the gun down. "He's your son, for Christ's sake."

I feel the cold of my father's stare as his eyes remain locked on mine. "You're nothin' more to me than a waste of cum." My father presses the end of the barrel a little harder into my forehead, his nostrils flaring and chest heaving. Eventually, he lowers the gun, bringing it up again and cracking me across the face. I stumble to the floor, tears collecting from the pain. My mom rushes over and throws her body around me like a shield. The hate I feel for my father has me lifting my head and locking eyes with him, thinking one day I will put a bullet in his head.

I wake, drenched in sweat and overwhelmed with anger and hate. I feel the same turmoil I felt when I was nine years old.

I stare at the ceiling, focusing on one of the fan blades as it slowly circulates clockwise. My emotions ripple through my body like waves crashing against a shoreline.

Giving up on sleep, I climb out of bed and drag my tired ass into the bathroom. I flip the switch on the wall, and the overhead light flickers a few times before staying lit. My room here at the clubhouse isn't huge, and neither is the bathroom, but it's far better than the concrete room Grey and I used to bunk in together when we were prospecting, so I sure as shit won't complain.

I reach behind the shower curtain and turn on the water. While steam fills the small bathroom, I rid myself of the sweatpants I sleep in and step into the shower stall beneath the stream of near-scalding water. I press my palms against the wall, hanging my head. As the water pelts my skin, it relaxes my muscles, and I release some of the tension my body is still holding. I hate that my past still has so much control over me, when I have fought so damn hard to bury it.

Closing my eyes, I think about the things in my life that ground me: my sobriety, the club, and all the success I'm experiencing with my artwork. Then Ember floods my thoughts, and the image of her standing in front of me in that tiny, cropped shirt and barely-there panties. Reaching down, I fist my cock and imagine everything I'd do to her if she were mine: her tits in my hands, taut nipples in my mouth. I would have her sit on my face as I feasted on her pussy before fucking her until she came on my dick.

A tingling sensation shoots up my spine, and my thigh muscles ripple as my release reaches its peak. A primal growl leaves my body as the orgasm rips through me. I give my cock a few more strokes before loosening the choke hold I have on it. "Fuck." Pulling in a ragged breath, I lean my head back, allowing the water to stream over my face. How pathetic am I? I'm reduced to rubbing one out in the shower, because I won't confess how I feel to Ember.

I shower until the water runs cold before turning it off. With a towel wrapped around my hips, I stand in front of the fogged-up mirror and swipe my hand across the surface a few times until I see a less hazy reflection. I stare at myself for several minutes, hating that I resemble my father. It's like his cold, blank eyes are staring back at me.

Never forget that you are loved, Blake. Don't listen to anyone who tells you otherwise. You, my son, are meant for greatness. You must always believe in yourself. These were the words my mom told me the day my father told me I was nothing more than a waste of cum.

A pounding at my bedroom door, followed by Grey's gruff voice calling my name, pulls me from intrusive thoughts. I stroll from the bathroom toward the door. "Blake," Grey barks again, his urgent tone setting me on high alert. I fling the bedroom door open. "Prez called. Someone broke into the garage."

Rushing, I toss the towel to the floor and dig out jeans and a shirt from the basket of clean clothes sitting on a chair in the corner. "Police on the scene?" I pull on my jeans and slip a black shirt over my head, then snatch a pair of socks from the same basket and begin putting on my boots.

"Yeah. Reid is there now, since he lives the closest, but Prez wants our asses down there until he makes it to town. We'll start our investigation while Reid handles the authorities. A fallen tree, caused by the storm that blew through here last night, is blocking the road at the end of his property, so he's dealing with that first."

"What's going on?"

I lift my head from tying my boots on hearing Ember's voice. She and Raine are standing just behind Grey in the hallway. "Break-in at the bike shop." I stand and take a few steps toward the dresser, retrieve my weapon, still in the holster, and clip it on the waistband of my jeans. Then I shove my wallet and keys into my pockets and snatch my cut from the hook on the wall. "Ready."

"That makes it the third business in town this month to be burglarized," Raine states. "You'd think the police would have a lead on who is behind them by now."

Grey steps to the side as I exit the bedroom. My eyes fall upon Ember for a moment. When her eyes lock with mine, I quickly divert my attention elsewhere, heading downstairs. Before closing the door, I look over my shoulder, finding the women, who have followed close behind. "Keep the place locked up until one of us gets back." My attention falls directly on Ember one final time before the door closes, and I walk away after hearing the locks engage.

It's windy as hell outside, and the ground is boggy from the earlier rainstorm. I meet Grey where our bikes are parked beneath the large metal carport Reid had his men build a few months ago. I toss my leg over the seat and look at Grey. "Let's ride."

A short time later, we roll up to the bike shop just as a police cruiser drives away. I notice Reid standing outside, holding a flashlight and talking on the phone. I also note that the streetlight that usually lights up the parking lot is out. Pulling up close to the entrance of the building, Grey and I leave our bikes and stand near Reid, waiting for him to get off the phone. "That was Prez." Reid looks at us. "He's still working on clearing the fallen tree off his property so he can leave. And there's no word yet on when they'll restore power."

I continue to stay vigilant and glance around the dark parking lot. "I expected to see more than one cop."

"The motherfuckers were long gone by the time of the discovery," Reid states. "That was officer Carver that just left. While on patrol through town, he noticed our exterior lights out and decided to investigate with the other business break-ins in mind."

I pull a cigarette from the pack tucked inside the pocket of my cut, drag my thumb across the wheel of a lighter, and hold the flame to the tip, burning the tobacco while Reid continues to fill us in.

"The motherfuckers drilled out the locking mechanism on the safe and made off with the money, and Prez says it was more than ten grand."

I expel the smoke from my lungs. "Fuck."

Reid jerks his head and leads us around the side of the

building, shining his light on the main breaker box, where the wires are severed.

"Well, that explains how they got in without setting off the alarm," Grey huffs.

We make our way to the back of the building, and Reid shines the flashlight on the door where the fuckers drilled off the deadbolt. The three of us step inside. During the walkthrough, I notice nothing disturbed or out of place except the empty cash drawer behind the counter, until we get to Jake's office. It's ransacked, and the safe is open.

"You think the fuckers realize who they stole from?" Grey quips, using the light from his phone to look around.

"They're about to." I pick up the papers scattered across the floor.

"From what Carver told me, the other town break-ins are similar: power cut to the building and locks drilled out. In each incident, they took nothing but cash. He also informed me that these motherfuckers are suspected to be behind several more break-ins in a few other towns. One job didn't go according to plan, resulting in the thieves shooting and killing a guy." Reid sighs. "Leave the mess. Let's focus on securing the back door for now and making a sweep of the property one more time. Prez said he's already sent word to the rest of the men to be at the clubhouse by sunrise. He also wants us to ride around, see if we see anything or anyone, and check on the other club businesses."

A few hours later, everyone is at the clubhouse, sitting around the table as Church commences. Looking tired and stressed, Jake leans back in his chair, working on his third cup of coffee since arriving. "The shop's power should be restored by late afternoon, and Reid's men are installing a new door as we speak." Jake rubs his temples, and agitation is evident. The last time anything crime related affected the shop was a few years ago when the place burned to the ground. It took time, but the club finally rebuilt. Jake leans forward, pounding his fist on the table with a loud thud. "These bastards stole from us. If the cops can't find out who's behind it, we will." Around the table, heads nod in agreement. Jake directs his attention to Quinn. "Did the outside security cameras catch anything before the thieves cut the power?"

"We only have the two fixed on the front and back doors. The broken streetlight hindered seeing anything farther than a few yards from the front of the building. Our outside cameras didn't detect anything beforehand. They used this to their advantage and most likely entered the property from the side, where they cut the power."

Jake faces Reid. "What did you find out?"

"Nothing new yet. I've contacted a few people who will report back with anything of value."

Jake nods, then peers at Gabriel. "See if your outside security cameras captured anything since you're across the street." Jake sits silently for a beat, rocking back in his chair, tapping his fingertips against the table's surface. "We know the pattern in which they operate, so let's put some extra security in place for Kings Custom, Kings Ink, Grace's bakery, and Kings Construction."

"What about trail cams?" Sam suggests. "We have extras stored down in the basement."

"Good thinkin'. You and Grey can get to installing those today. If you need more, run to the sporting goods store, pick some up, and tell Pat to charge it to the club's account." Jake stands. "There's a hot meal waiting for us in the kitchen. Cram some grub, and let's get shit done." With Church over, we file out of the room.

My stomach growls as the smell of bacon permeates the air, invading my senses. I make my way to the kitchen and take a deep breath. "Smells good." Ember looks over her shoulder and smiles at me.

"Hey. Want some coffee? I just brewed a fresh pot."

"Thanks." I walk over to the table, pull a chair, and sit down. Across the table, Quinn is shoveling biscuits and gravy into his mouth. Ember sets a cup of coffee and a plate of food in front of me. I glance up, and she looks exhausted. "You eat?" I ask her.

"Not yet."

I stand. "Sit." I point to the chair.

"That's okay. I'll eat after everyone else."

I stare at her until she caves.

"Fine," she huffs, taking the seat I vacated. "You need to eat too," she fusses.

I stroll over to the spread of food placed on the counter, grab a plate, and pile on bacon, biscuits with gravy, and scrambled eggs, then return, taking a seat beside Ember. Giving me a soft smile, Ember picks up her fork and eats. Across the table, Quinn chews his food, staring at me with the same grin he gives whenever there's open interaction between Ember and me. Quinn says nothing. He doesn't have to. I know what he's thinking. All of them are waiting for me to stake my claim on Ember.

Our friendship works for us as-is. At least, that's what I keep trying to convince myself.

4

EMBER

Alderman Phillip Rhoads Announces Candidacy for Governor of Georgia

I close the laptop without bothering to read beyond the article's headline. Whatever the media wrote isn't anything I don't already know. My sister texted me yesterday with the news. She also told me the reporter who came to the house to interview my father inquired about the eldest Rhoads daughter. Scarlett said Dad deflected like he always does. Over the years, my parents have done an excellent job lying about their daughter and what she's been up to. As far as the public knows, Bailey Rhoads lives abroad. While volunteering one summer, I fell in love with Europe and decided to stay. What a fucking cliché. But it's not like I expect Phillip and Caroline Rhoads to disclose their daughter currently resides in Montana with a well-known motorcycle club.

Not even their closest friends know. If it got out that Bailey Rhoads was a club girl for Kings of Retribution and what that entails, it would ruin my parents' reputation and my father's political career. I'm the well-hidden black sheep of the family. When I was a child, my parents had my future mapped out. Bailey Ember Rhoads was destined for greatness. But I never wanted to be great. I only ever wanted to be me. Instead, I got a childhood filled with loneliness, private schools, tutors, and enough extracurricular activities to fill every second of my free time from when I was seven until I decided to leave.

It wasn't until I met Jake and the club that I found an actual family dynamic that I fell in love with. With the Kings, I'm free to be whoever I wish to be. That's not to say I don't face judgment from the outside world. To outsiders, I'm no more than a whore. Sure, other clubs refer to their women as whores but not the Kings. To them, I'm a club girl. I'm respected and never treated with anything less than kindness. The same goes for the other club girl Raine. However, the most important aspect of club life is loyalty.

Jake runs his club with an iron fist and demands respect and devotion from all who step foot onto Kings' territory and from those he lets into his club. Over the years, people have tested the boundaries, and they didn't live to regret their choices.

Two of whom were former club girls. All that remain are Raine and me. As far as I know, Jake has yet to make plans to add to the family by bringing in more women. All the brothers, aside from Blake and Grey, are settled down and married. As each man found the love of his life and started a family, I became increasingly worried about my role in the club. I'm terrified of losing the people I consider family. Grace, Bella, Alba, Mila, Emerson, and Lelani accept Raine and me and have from day one. I have an unspoken rule: the club's members become off-limits when one of the brothers finds a woman.

It was only a short time after Austin brought Lelani to the club that Jake caught me looking at apartment listings one afternoon.

. . .

"What ya doin', sweetheart?" Jake strolls up behind me, where I'm sitting at the bar, and looks over my shoulder at my laptop.

"Oh, I'm just looking at apartments." I try for a nonchalant shrug. Jake freezes, turns me on my stool, and pins me with a stare. "Come again?"

I try holding eye contact, but I can't. I begin to fidget in my seat. A few days ago, I decided it was time to move out. Moving out of the clubhouse breaks my heart, but it's time.

"Eyes, Ember." Jake's tone is gentle yet firm. He remains silent as I lift my eyes to his. "My office, now." Jake walks ahead, and I hop off the stool and follow. He rounds his desk and sits as I sit on one of the chairs in front of him. I wait while he lights a cigarette, takes a drag, and leans back in the chair. "You want to tell me why you're looking at apartments?"

I rub my palms along my denim-covered thighs. "I was thinking it's time."

Jake takes another drag. "Because?"

"Well, because...there's no reason to stay. You know."

The chair squeaks under Jake's weight as he shifts forward. "No reason to stay? Are you not happy here, Ember?" Now his tone is one of concern.

"No, no! I've never been happier. I love living here."

Jake squints. "Then what's the problem?"

"There's no problem." My throat begins to close, and I can feel the tears threatening to spill at any moment.

"Darlin', what's this really about?" Jake asks.

"It's just. Maybe it's not right for me to be here anymore." I sniffle.

A light goes on in Jake's head, and I see the moment what I'm talking about dawns on him. He snubs his cigarette, stands, walks around the desk, and squats down in front of me. "Ember, you're family."

"I know, but—"

He cuts me off. "Over the years, the dynamics of the club have changed, but the foundation remains, sweetheart. We are family, and there will never be a time you aren't welcome in this family. Do you understand?"

I nod. "Yes."

"Now I'm going to ask you a question, and I want the truth."

"Okay."

"Do you want to move out of the clubhouse?"

I sniffle again and shake my head.

Jake stands. "It's settled then."

That was the end of the conversation between Jake and me about my moving out. Thinking about that day also brings back the memory of the fight Blake and I had later that night. He'd gotten wind of my plans and lost his shit. Closing my eyes, I shake off the memory and all thoughts of Blake, because everything about us is complicated. Right now, I need to focus on the disaster at hand: my parents.

Picking up my cell, I call my sister. She answers on the second ring.

"Hey."

I blow out a breath and flop back in my bed. "I just saw the announcement."

"Mom is making me come home."

I sit up. "But you're in the middle of your semester."

Scarlett blows out a breath. "I know. She says she and Dad need me."

"They just want to parade you around for Dad's campaign."

"I know, but what choice do I have, Ember?"

"You have a choice, Scar. What does Keith have to say?"

Keith is the guy my sister is secretly dating. He's a mechanic and five years older than her. They're head over heels for each other, and my sister has never been happier. Our parents would shit bricks if they found out about him.

"It's not that easy, sis. And I haven't told Keith yet."

"Scar."

"I'll figure something out. Don't worry about me."

Scarlett is in her second semester of college in North Carolina. My little sister is the timid and shy sister out of us two. She doesn't know how to stand up to our parents. She was still little when I left and never showed her how to endure the pressures and expectations they dish out. I carry guilt with me every day, knowing she's miserable.

After I left, they pushed Scarlett the same way they did me, demanding perfection from her, knowing she wasn't like me. Scarlett has dyslexia, but our parents refuse to acknowledge it. I didn't communicate with my sister for three years after leaving home because my parents forbade it. Then one day, when she was thirteen, I called the private school she was attending, pretending to be our mom. I'll never forget hearing my little sister's voice for the first time after so long. We spoke long enough for me to give her my number. That was the beginning of our secret relationship. Things were going great until Mom found the gift I sent for her sixteenth birthday. I remember getting a call, expecting it to be my sister. Instead, my mother's scornful voice demanded I never speak to Scarlett again.

After that, they disconnected my sister's phone. Almost one month later, I received a call from an unknown number in the middle of the night. It was Scarlett. Our parents had pulled her from private school and sent her to boarding school. She pleaded with another student to use their phone and called me. Scarlett is older now, but she is still very much under their thumbs. I don't blame her, though. I blame them. My parents' number one priority always has been and always will be their reputation and my father's career. One positive thing I can say is my baby sister is changing, and I have Keith to thank for that. She has blossomed since being with him. I can only hope my support and her love for Keith will be enough for her to break away from our parents' hold on her.

"Look, I'm meeting Keith for lunch. I'll call you tomorrow."

"All right. Talk later. I love you, Scar."

"Love you too."

After hanging up with my sister, I check the time. It's after midnight, but, knowing I won't get any sleep with everything on my mind, I check my email. Grabbing my laptop, I cross my legs and set it on my thighs. As expected, I have an email from Alice asking when she can expect my next manuscript. I type out a quick response letting her know she can expect it by the end of the week, six days before my deadline. I smile and shake my head. Alice is just as anxious for the next Montana Nights book as my readers.

For the next hour, I check all my socials and answer a few reader questions. I'm still blown away at what my life has become in the past year-and-a-half. I wasn't much of a reader until Alba and Leah roped me into joining their book club. Two chapters into the first romance novel, I was hooked. It didn't take long for me to start conjuring up my own stories. One day, I started writing down all my ideas. Then I started thinking about *what if I wrote my own book?* One afternoon, I sat down with my computer, and the words poured out. I'd never typed so much in my life. It was very therapeutic. I discovered something in myself that had been missing.

Over a few weeks, I wrote over 300 pages, had my first rough draft, and needed help figuring out where to go from there. So, I joined several online support groups, and with their help figured out the tools I needed to self-publish my story. And I did just that. I published the first book in my Montana Nights series, under the pen name Ellise Brooks, a year and a half ago. The series follows four brothers who are cowboys that live on a ranch in a small town, overcoming their trials and tribulations to find love.

I remember how nervous I was during the launch of my first book. I didn't have any high expectations for it. I would have been happy if only one person read and loved it. And I'm not going to lie; I started to doubt myself and my ability to write a good story for the first few months. Then one day I got online to see book sales exploding. It's true when they say success can happen overnight. Now here I am, about to finish my fourth book. The real kicker is nobody knows. I mean, no one. Not the club, not the girls, not even my sister. Honestly, it's a goddamn miracle I haven't spilled the beans to Alba and Leah yet.

I chuckle to myself. Bailey Ember Rhoads, who graduated high school at thirteen and graduated college at eighteen with a double major in business and political science, writes smut.

5

BLAKE

A loud pop wakes me from sleep. My room is shrouded in darkness. Fear paralyzes me as I stare into the hallway through the crack of my bedroom door because Mom knows I like it left open just a little. Something doesn't feel right. I try to swallow, but my mouth is dry. I hear my granddad shouting but can't make out the words over the sound of my heartbeat drumming in my ears as panic grips my insides. Suddenly, Mom rushes into my bedroom. The smell of her lily perfume engulfs me as she uncovers me. "It's going to be alright," she whispers, pulling me out of bed. She leads me to the closet. "I need you to stay in the closet, Vita Mia. And no matter what you hear, promise me you won't move."

"Wait. Where are you going?" I get up from the far corner of the closet, where Mom sat me down.

"Blake." Mom's assertiveness doesn't mask the fearful undertone in her voice. "No matter what. Promise me."

I'm only ten, but I know something is wrong, and that what is happening terrifies her. "I promise." I whisper the words she needs to hear without realizing the magnitude of the situation.

"I love you, Blake. I will always be with you." Before I can tell her "I

love you" in return, Mom quickly closes the door, and I'm sitting in pitch dark. All I can hear is myself breathing.

Another popping sound shatters the silence, and I realize it's a gunshot, which is soon followed by another. My heart thunders inside my chest, and my chest tightens, making breathing hard.

"Hudson, please. I'm begging you, please don't do this!" my mom cries. What is my father doing here? I need to protect my mom. It's the only thought going through my head right now, knowing my father is in the house. I reach for the door handle but hesitate. I promised. Another gunshot rings out, followed by two blood-curdling screams from my mother and grandma.

I break my promise and bolt out of the closet, then rush out of my bedroom. Another gunshot rings out before I reach the steps leading downstairs. My mom wails, a rough, guttural sound I've never heard before. "Please, please. Don't do this." Her voice breaks between words.

"You stole from me—from the club." My father's voice sounds hard.

"Please, Hudson. I'll pay you back every penny," my mom continues pleading, choking on her voice.

"You belong to me," my father spews.

"You don't love me, Hudson. Let me go!" Mom cries.

I stumble on the last step and land hard on my stomach, barely stopping my face from smacking against the hard floor. I'm instantly aware of wetness beneath me and lift my hand, only to see my palm covered in a thin layer of red liquid. I push up, kneeling and staring at the tiny blood pool. My gaze travels, landing on my grandpa, and lying motionless beside him is my grandma. My body begins to tremble uncontrollably.

"Blake!" my mom shouts, but her voice sounds far away. "Blake run!" she screams as I'm roughly jerked sideways and brought to my feet.

"Get over here, you little shit," my father spits, fisting the collar of my shirt. Suddenly I'm before my mom, who is kneeling.

I struggle against my father's hold, swinging my fists and landing an ineffective blow to his gut before getting my body in a position where I successfully kick him in the balls.

My father grunts, "Motherfucker." The gun in his other hand is now pressing against the side of my head.

"No, Hudson. Please." Mom's red, tear-stained eyes dart between my father and me. Her hands clutch her chest. "Blake has done nothing wrong. I'm to blame. I love you. I'll do better—I'll be better," she begs. Her head jerks to the side, her gaze focusing elsewhere. I look in the direction her attention is focused and spot another club member.

My father shoves me toward his club brother. "Control the kid."

He's much larger than me, but I fight against his hold anyway. Throwing punches earns me a man-sized fist to the gut, and I double over, the pain from the blow making me vomit. The club member laughs and yanks my hair. "You move again; I kill you." He puts a blade on my neck.

My father moves closer to my mom, his gun aimed at her face, and she closes her eyes. "I'm begging you. He's your son, Hudson. He hasn't lived. Please do what you want with me but don't take that away from him. If you have any love for me, don't take his future away from him."

My stomach coils because Mom sounds like she's giving up. "Mom!" I bellow. "Mom, fight back," I implore.

My father looks back at me, his eyes locking with mine, face smirking. His expression hardens, devoid of emotion. Before my eyes, he turns into something else—something evil. He turns back to face my mom. "I'll spare his life," he tells her, and her shoulders sag in relief.

Mom opens her eyes, looks up at my dad, then turns and looks at me. "I love you, Vita Mia."

A gunshot follows her words.

My eyes snap open, and I jackknife up in bed. Breaking out in a cold sweat, I'm breathless and my heart is pounding. I scrub my hand over my face, shaking off the adrenaline and lingering emotions. Attempting to get my bearings, I take in a deep breath to slow my heart rate. Once most of the nightmare's side effects subside, I leave bed and head for the bathroom, where I lean over the sink and splash cold water on my face. Knowing I won't go back to sleep again, I throw a t-shirt on with my sweatpants and quietly go downstairs and into the kitchen to make coffee.

With a mug of the steaming liquid in hand, I step outside onto the back deck, then grab a chair and sit facing east. I sip my coffee while breathing in the cool morning air, waiting for the sun to rise. The door behind me slides open, and I'm soon joined by Ember, with her body wrapped in a blanket, holding her own cup of coffee. I drag a chair over for her to sit beside me.

"Can't sleep?" She sits, tucking the blanket around her legs.

"Nightmare," I confess, since she knows I have them anyway.

"Want to talk about it?"

"It's bad enough I live with the fucked up memories, babe. Not going to share them with others." My body still feels tense, and the final gunshot rings in my ears.

Ember sighs. "Sometimes talking about it helps."

I stare at the sky, watching the horizon line change from dark blue into a crimson glow. Calm washes over me. I breathe in deeply again. Brushstrokes of purple, orange, and yellow begin painting the sky. I glance at Ember, taking in her profile as she watches the start of a new day. The wind blows, and she closes her eyes, feeling the breeze caress her skin. In the warmth of the sunrise, golden hues kiss her face. She takes my breath away. First thing in the morning, with her hair all a mess and not a stitch of makeup on, is when I find Ember the most beautiful. As she turns my way, I look at the sky.

"If you don't want to share bad memories, how about good ones?"

Right away, my grandparents come to mind. Those few months living with them were some of my life's happiest, carefree moments. "My grandparents lived on a small farm outside of San Bernardino, had a huge vegetable garden and a couple of cows." I take a sip of my coffee. "Rural life was different, in a good way." I lean back and sink into the good memories that get buried by the bad. "It's probably why I like Montana so much." I think about being in the kitchen with my mom and grandma as they made homemade butter from heavy cream. "Every Sunday, my grandma would be in the kitchen cookin' a spread of food: grilled vegetables, zucchini fritters, risotto, and Roulade. I listened to her and my grandfather talk about growing up on small farms in Italy. They were childhood sweethearts who dreamed of living in America. A year after they married, they fulfilled that dream." The wind blows, and I can almost smell the memory.

"They never questioned why we just showed up at their doorstep with no phone call or warning. They wrapped their arms around us and told my mom, Viviana, 'I'm so happy you are home.'" I fall silent for a beat, trying to keep rooted in the present, but I feel myself slipping into the bitter anger from having all the good stolen from me all those years ago. For a moment in my life, though brief, I got to experience being a normal kid without carrying the world's weight on my shoulders. More importantly, my mom was happy and free and I hadn't seen her that way in a very long time. I close my eyes and remember how beautiful my mom was. "If I could go back and rewrite history, I would. They didn't deserve to die."

"What about your mom? What was she like?"

I smile thinking about her and warmth spreads through my chest. "Despite loving my father, she was a good woman and a great mom. For all the love I never received from my father, she made up for it tenfold. She loved flowers, roses being her favorite. And she was a hard worker. She worked a waitress job at a small diner a few blocks from where we lived. I used to hang out there all the time when I wasn't in school." I chuckle a little, thinking about Mrs. Maggie, the owner. "When my mom wasn't looking, the sweet old lady, Mrs. Maggie, would slip me money, usually five rolled-together one-dollar bills that she kept in her apron pocket. Then she'd tell me to go across the street and get myself some soda and some candy. If my mom knew, she never let on to the fact."

I grow silent and Ember reaches out, resting her hand atop mine, lacing our fingers together. Her touch becomes my lifeline, keeping me afloat. She says nothing. We sit in the stillness of the beginning of a new day. I can't help wanting more between us, wishing I had something to offer her other than the broken pieces that make me who I am.

It's the end of the day, and we're all out here at the bar, enjoying greasy bar food, good music, and great company while celebrating Charley's birthday.

After winning another game of pool against Grey, I nurse a beer and cut my eyes across the bar to Ember. She's been perched at the bar, chatting it up with some fucker I haven't seen before. My core temperature rises, watching the prick lean in close and whisper something in her ear that causes Ember to throw her head back laughing. I don't like it. My grip on the bottle tightens.

Grey stands beside me, a beer in his hand. "Who pissed in your Cheerios?" He follows my line of sight. "Just tell her how you feel, brother."

"Nothing to tell," I lie. Grey gives me a side-eye. "Lie to someone else fucker. I'm your best friend, and I know shit." I glare at him, and he throws his hands up. "I know the drill, but she won't wait forever, brother." Grey walks off, leaving me to sulk.

I pull out an empty chair at a nearby table and sit, keeping my eyes on Ember. I don't like being jealous of a stranger, but right now, I am. I look down at the beer in my hand and use the excuse that I could use another one to stand and make my way toward the bar. I slide in behind Ember, deliberately brushing my shoulder against hers while making eye contact with the guy talking to her.

"There a problem?" The guy stares me down, clearly irritated at my presence. Bold motherfucker; I'll give him that. I ignore him and lift my empty beer bottle, signaling to Kinsley behind the counter that I'm ready for another.

Pencil Dick leans into Ember and rests his hand on her bare thigh. "What do you say we get out of here?"

Heat spreads through my body at the thought of Ember leaving with this shithead. I clench my fists against the bar top, dangling on the breath that I'm holding, waiting to hear Ember's reply.

"I'll have to pass." Ember turns him down, and I relax my hands.

"Come on, sweet thing. Let me show you a good time."

"She said no," I growl.

The prick sneers. "Mind your business, bro."

I push back from the bar.

"Blake." Ember slides from her barstool and looks at me, but I stare past her, my attention elsewhere. "Don't."

I move Ember gently but firmly out of the way, grab the bastard by the back of the head, and slam his face into the bar top. "She is my fuckin' business. She's mine. And I'm not your bro." I back off, hoping he'll come at me for more.

"I don't see any ring on the bitch's finger." He spits blood at my feet and then wipes his busted lip with the back of his hand. He throws a punch, and I stand still, letting him have the first blow. His knuckles clip my chin.

I swing, landing a fist on the side of his head, and he stumbles. Giving him no time to recover, I land another blow to his head, and he falls to his knees. I keep going, kicking him in the ribs.

Large arms wrap around me, pulling me back. "Enough!" Gabriel snaps, holding me as the cocksucker gets to his feet.

"No piece of ass is worth this much trouble." He spits at my feet again and walks out of the bar.

"Well, I guess no birthday is complete without a bar fight," Charley announces. "Show is over, people. Get back to drinking and spending your money, or go home."

Gabriel releases his hold on me and slaps me on the back before returning to his woman.

Ember approaches, her pretty face twisted with anger. "I can't believe you did that. And on Charley's birthday," she hisses. "I can take care of myself."

"The fucker wasn't willing to take no for an answer."

Ember crosses her arm and cocks her head. "You're jealous."

"I was lookin' out for you."

"Bullshit. You were looking out for yourself. You don't own me, Blake. And until you decide I am worth wanting, you don't get the right to act as if I belong to you." She stomps away.

A hand firmly grips my shoulder, preventing me from going after her. "Come on," Jake orders, and I comply, following him to a secluded corner of the bar, where we sit at a table away from everyone.

"You here to give me shit about Ember too?" I say, instantly regretting the clipped tone of my voice.

Jake ignores the burst of attitude. "She's not mad, son. She's hurt. You can't keep giving her mixed signals. You got to tell her how you feel or cut her loose. Staying stuck in the in-between is no way to live. You both deserve better than that."

"As bad as I want Ember, I'm no good for her."

Jake studies me for a beat. "Why?"

"I'm fucked up, Prez. How can I give Ember the future she deserves if I can't move on from the past? My father is permanently embedded in my head. The only time I don't hear his voice telling me what a worthless piece of shit I am is when I'm using." I shake my head. "I can't ask Ember to take on that burden."

Jake studies me. "Your sobriety becoming an issue?"

"No," is my quick response. "You have my word."

Jake nods, noting the sincerity in my words. "None of us are without flaws. And fuck your father. The bastard is dead."

I cut my eyes at him. "Yeah, and I killed him," I mutter.

"Yes; you did. But son, you can't live your life looking back all the time, or you'll continue to miss what's right in front of you." Jake crosses his arms over his chest. "Let me ask you this. Would you be willing to carry Ember's burdens? Because I'm telling you right now, she has her own heavy shit weighing her down. "

"I'd do anything for Ember. I'd cut off my own goddamn arm if she asked me to," I say vehemently.

"What makes you think she wouldn't want to do the same? Sounds to me like you're trying to make that decision for her."

When I don't say anything, Jake continues, "Sooner or later, Ember's going to move on. She's going to find a man willing to give her all the things you want but are too chicken-shit to get off the pot."

My jaw ticks and my fists clench at the thought of Ember with another man.

"That's what I thought." Jake uncrosses his arms and stands. "I think you have all the answers you need, son." He claps my shoulder and retreats to the opposite corner of the room to join Grace.

I glance around the bar, taking in all the people in my life enjoying the rest of the night, drinking and laughing. My eyes land on Ember, sitting with Bella and Alba while they watch Logan and Gabriel shoot a game of pool. Sensing my watchful presence, Ember turns her head, making eye contact with me. I mouth *I'm a dick,* and even though she shoots daggers at me, her anger quickly dissipates and she smiles.

Jake is right. I need to get my head out of my ass.

6

EMBER

"You got a minute?" Jake raps his knuckles on the bar and sits across from where I'm wiping down the bar and restocking.

"Sure. What's up?" I wipe my hands on a rag and pop open a soda. "Want one?" I ask.

"I'll take a beer if you don't mind, darlin'."

I twist the cap off a beer and slide it before him. "What's on your mind?"

"I saw the news about your old man the other day and wanted to see where your head was on all that."

I shrug. "I'm fine, and the lie about where I've been all these years still seems to work for them." It suddenly dawns on me why Jake is showing concern. "Why? Do you think the press will question my parents and decide to start snooping around? Because if you're worried about that, I promise I won't let any unwanted attention make its way to the club," I'm quick to say.

"Ember, darlin'." Jake clears his throat. "I don't give a fuck about any of that. Dealing with nosy-ass reporters is the furthest thing from my mind. I want to know how *you* are doing."

My shoulders slump, and I exhale a sigh of relief. "I'm sorry, Jake."

"Nothin' to be sorry for, sweetheart."

I nod. "The truth is; I'm worried about my sister."

Jake's brow furrows with concern. "She okay?"

"We talked after I read the news of my dad's big announcement. They want her to leave school and come home to be a dutiful daughter. And she agreed." I walk around the bar and sit beside him. "I don't know what I'm going to do, Jake. She doesn't need them. I told her I would pay for school or whatever else she needs. But our parents have this sick hold on her, and I can't figure it out. I mean, she's miserable when she's home. At school, she's happy. Then there is her boyfriend. She's blossomed so much under his attention. I know she will shrink back into herself when she returns home."

Jake grips my neck, leaving me no choice but to look at him. "Listen, Ember. There is nothin' more you can do to help your sister. You offered the tools she needs to get out of the fucked-up situation she's in. It's up to her to accept. Be patient, and she'll come around."

I shake my head, disagreeing with his words. "She's not strong enough."

"Darlin', if your sister has even one ounce of her big sister running through her veins, then she's strong enough."

I bite my bottom lip. "You think so?"

Jake stands and kisses the top of my head. "I know so. Besides, we all have our breaking points. Eventually, those fucks will drive your sister to hers. And when they do, her sister will have her back, and so will the club."

I close my eyes and try to hold back my emotions. This is why I love Jake and what makes him the best man I know. "Thank you," I whisper.

"Anytime, Ember," he replies softly.

I stand and return to stocking the bar, then he asks, "Any plans for the day?"

"Not really. Why? Did you need me for something?"

"Yeah. I promised Grace dinner and a ride up the mountain on my bike tonight, but our sitter canceled on us, and Remi is sleeping over at a friend's house. I was going to see if you could watch Ellie Kate for us."

I smile. "I'd love to. What time do you need me?"

"Don't know what I'd do without ya, sweetheart. Can you be at the house by six?"

"I'll be there."

Just then, Grace walks through the door of the clubhouse. "Hey, baby. What are ya doin' here? Is everything okay?" Jake strides over to his woman.

"Everything is fine. Remi called and said she left her laptop in your office and asked if I could bring it to Kenzi's house. They're going to work on that science project together." When Grace spots me, she gives me a huge smile. "Hey, Ember. How are you?"

"Good. I was talking to your husband and told him I'd be at your place this evening to watch Ellie."

"Oh, Ember. You are a godsend." Grace practically skips over to me and hugs my neck. "Things have been so hectic lately with the kids and the bakery that I'm dying for a few hours of stress-free adult time. You know what I mean?" She laughs.

"I know what you mean." I wink. "Don't worry, I got you."

In the afternoon, I'm sitting at the desk in my room writing when someone knocks at the door. "Yeah?" I call out without looking away from the computer. "The door's open."

"Hey." Alba steps through with Leah trailing behind.

I shut my laptop and look over my shoulder. "Hey yourself."

Alba and Leah plop down on the bed. "So, we have some news," Leah says.

I turn in my chair. "Oh. What's up?"

The two friends look at each other with big smiles and then back at me. Alba speaks up. "Leah and I have decided to open a bookstore."

"Are you serious!?"

"Completely!" Leah can barely contain her excitement.

Alba adds, "Well, you know we've mentioned a time or two how cool it would be if we did, so Leah and I got to talking, and we figured, why not."

I jump up. "Oh my god! This is great!"

"I know!" Alba gushes. "I can't believe we're going to do it."

"It's going to be amazing." I pull Alba in for a hug. "And don't be afraid to ask me for help. Seriously, whatever you two need."

"We're glad you offered." Leah stands. "Because we wanted to ask if you'd come with us to look at a possible space for the store. We have to meet the realtor in thirty minutes."

"I'd love to. Just let me put my shoes on and grab my purse." I spot my boots beside the bed. "Where's it at?"

"It's that empty building down the sidewalk from the bakery," Alba tells me.

"Oh, the place that used to be a flower shop?" I grab my purse from the back of my chair.

"That's the one," Leah chirps.

Blake pulls up on his motorcycle just as we exit the clubhouse and approach Leah's car. The girls smile and wave, which earns them a nod. "Ladies."

I, on the other hand, keep my eyes forward and my feet moving. That doesn't stop me from feeling Blake's heated gaze burning a hole in the back of my head.

"What was that all about?" Alba boldly asks once we get on the road.

I pretend not to know what she's talking about. "What?"

Alba rolls her eyes. "You suck at playing dumb, Ember."

I sigh. "It was nothing."

"Sure didn't seem like nothing," Leah mutters.

"Blake is complicated."

"Well, no shit," Alba snorts. "The man is a mystery, and he's also wound tighter than anyone I know." Alba twists in her seat. "The way that man looked at you back there had me blushing."

I snort. "You're crazy."

Luckily the subject of Blake and me is dropped, and a short time later, we pull up to the building where Alba and Leah are meeting the realtor. I will admit it makes me feel special.

"So." The woman who has spent thirty minutes showing us around the space clasps her hands together. "What do you ladies think?"

I smile at Leah and Alba. "By the look on your faces, I'd say this is it."

"What do you think?" Alba asks me directly.

"It's perfect. I especially love the open window space at the front, which gives the right amount of natural light. You can put a big comfy sofa and a table there." I walk over to where Leah is standing by a set of stairs. "And this loft space could serve as a reading nook. I mean, it can be whatever you two decide. I was only thinking out loud." I wave my hand, feeling embarrassed. "Ignore me."

"No, no." Alba steps forward. "I love your ideas. Leah and I want your opinion. That's why we asked you to tag along. Neither of us has your kind of style or vision."

I duck my head to hide my blush. "Oh, okay."

. . .

I'm walking into the bank an hour later with Alba and Leah when I ask, "What are we doing here?"

Leah answers first. "We have an appointment with Mr. Sinclair about a loan."

Confused, I ask, "A loan?"

"Yeah, for the store," Alba tells me.

I stop Alba just outside the entrance. "You're married to Gabriel. And you," I add, pointing to Leah, "are a Volkov."

Leah shrugs. "Alba and I decided we wanted to do this independently."

"Oh." I smile, but it quickly fades. "How'd your husbands take that?"

Leah snorts. "Nikolai was not happy."

"And Gabriel blew a fuse and tried to go all alpha on me," Alba adds.

"I bet." I can't hold back my giggle. "So, how did you two manage to get them to agree?"

The two women eye each other with grins and a knowing look, then say in unison, "We have our ways," followed by laughter.

I can see the moment Mr. Sinclair calls us into his pretentious office; he will be a problem.

"There's just not much I can do for you."

"But if—" Alba goes on to say only to have Mr. Sinclair cut her off.

"You, ladies, could apply again in a year. Or I suggest bringing your husbands down to apply for you. A loan this size—"

Having had enough of this sexist asshole bulldozing my girls, I interrupt him the same way he has done Leah and Alba each time they've tried to speak, from the moment we sat down. Without moving from my seat and with a calm tone, I ask, "What makes you think Mrs. Martinez and Mrs. Volkov can't financially handle a loan of that size, Mr. Sinclair?" I grin when his brow furrows in confusion at Leah's and Alba's married names. Everyone who works at this bank knows who the Volkovs and the Martinezes are.

"There must be some confusion. The names stated on the application are Winters and Jameson," he sputters. Judging by the sweat beading on his forehead, it clicked in his tiny little brain just who are sitting in his office.

"Those are mine and Alba's maiden names," Leah informs Mr. Sinclair.

"That's right," Alba adds. "The LLC for my graphic design business is under my maiden name, Jameson."

The prick behind the desk starts to sputter. "I...I'm sorry, Mrs. Martinez and Mrs. Volkov. I had no idea."

"Chad, what in the world is going on here?"

We all turn to the door to see Mr. Lawrence, who I know to be the President of Polson Regional Bank, standing in the open doorway of Mr. Sinclair's office.

"Nothing is going on, Mr. Lawrence. Just a little misunderstanding." Chad nervously laughs.

"Actually, Mr. Sinclair told Mrs. Martinez and Mrs. Volkov that he can't possibly approve them for the loan they very much qualify for."

"No, no. That's not—"

The asshole is cut off again by Alba. "That's exactly what happened. You barely glanced at our application, and then you insulted us by suggesting we have our husbands come down and do business with you."

"You know." I cut my eyes to Alba and Leah with a grin. "You should ask Nikolai and Gabriel to chat with Mr. Sinclair, after all."

"No." Mr. Lawrence rushes fully into the office. "That won't be necessary. Please, Mrs. Volkov and Mrs. Martinez, come to my office, and I will handle everything from here."

The three of us gather our things as a red-faced Mr. Lawrence turns back to his colleague. "Chad, you're fired."

. . .

After stopping for pizza and ice cream, I arrive at Jake and Grace's place ten minutes before six. "Hey, sweetheart. Come on in," Grace greets me while opening the door. I brace myself after hearing the squeal of laughter followed by Ellie running down the hall toward me. Luckily, Jake is there to grab the pizza from my hands before Ellie throws herself at my legs. "Ember!"

"Hey, munchkin." I scoop her up.

"Daddy said you were coming over, so I set up a tea party for us in my room."

"You did?"

Ellie nods her head vigorously.

"You know what goes good with tea?" I ask.

"Pizza!" she shouts.

"You know it." I kiss her cheek.

"Ellie Kate, why don't you put the ice cream in the freezer for Ember before it melts." Jake takes his little girl from my arms, kisses the top of her head, and sets her on her feet.

"Okay, daddy."

Once Ellie is out of earshot, Jake turns to me. "You spoil her."

I roll my eyes. "Like you don't."

He chuckles. "Can ya blame me?"

I laugh. "No."

When Jake's face turns serious, I hang my purse on the hook by the front door and give him my full attention. "What's wrong?"

"Heard what happened today with Alba and Leah."

"I figured you would." I sigh. "Look, I know it wasn't my place to butt in like I did, since I was only there for support because the girls wanted my opinion on the space they were going to look at, but that guy was a sexist jerk, and it wasn't sitting right with me."

"Ember—"

I put my hands on my hips and start to pace as I feel myself getting worked up again just from talking about it. "He knew the girls were more than qualified. Then he had to go and bring up that spiel about having their husbands come in for them."

"Ember." Jake places his hand on my shoulder, halting me in place. "You don't have to plead your case." His lip twitches. "I brought up the subject because I wanted to thank you for having Alba and Leah's back. I talked to Gabriel and Nikolai this afternoon, and both are grateful for what you did."

I breathe a sigh of relief. "Good. I don't ever want to overstep. Alba and Leah can speak for themselves, but that guy is an asshole."

"Oh, I heard. Gabriel said Alba wouldn't stop talkin' about how you put the son of a bitch in his place."

"Yeah?" I flash an award-winning smile.

"Yeah, darlin'." Jake squeezes my shoulder. "You did good today."

"Jake, honey, are you ready?" Grace walks into the room with Ellie trailing behind, holding a box. "Ember, thanks again for agreeing to watch Ellie Kate."

"Anytime, Grace. You two get out of here and have some fun." I turn my attention to Ellie. "What do you say we get this party started?"

"Yay! Will you play Candy Land with me?"

"Duh. Like you have to ask. You know Candy Land is my favorite."

Grace bends down and kisses her daughter. "You be good for Ember. Daddy and I will be back later."

"I will, Mommy."

Ellie and I stand on the porch and wave at Jake and Grace as they take off on his bike. Once they're out of view, I look down and hold out my hand. "Come on, kiddo. Candy Land and pizza are calling my name."

7

BLAKE

Gabriel and Grey left more than an hour ago, leaving me the only one left at the shop. The sun has already set, and I'm a few more strokes of the needle away from finishing up Prez's new ink he's getting to honor his woman and their children; a black and gray left chest piece of a lion with his lioness and two cubs. After several hours, I lean back, place my ink gun on the table, and clean the freshly finished tattoo. "Have a look," I instruct, while preparing the materials to cover it up. Jake gets off the table he's been stretched out on and strides over to the full-length mirror hanging on the wall.

He nods in approval. "Fuck, yeah. You killed it, brother." He walks back over, and I place the covering over his new ink. "Heard Ink Kings approached the shop, and they want to do a feature on the Kings Ink crew."

Ink Kings is a popular online magazine that shines a spotlight on tattoo artists and models from around the world and all walks of life. Gabriel got a call from one of their representatives this morning to offer us a spread in their next issue. "Yeah," I confirm. I finish cleaning my workstation, remove my disposable gloves, and toss them in the trash. "They want to interview each of us and showcase our artwork."

"Y'all deserve it." Jake extends his hand. "Thanks, son. I'm proud to wear your art on my skin permanently."

"Thanks, Prez." I clasp his hand, feeling grateful for his praise.

Jake throws his shirt on and shrugs his cut over his shoulders. "I've got to hit the head; then I'm outta here and heading to the bakery to follow Grace home." He heads for the restroom.

I gather the trash, step out the back door, and sling the bag into the dumpster. As I walk back inside and set the alarm, my phone rings. Why would Ember be calling me? I swipe the screen and bring the phone to my ear. "What's up?"

"Blake." Ember's voice is nothing more than a whisper but is filled with panic. "Someone just broke into the bakery." Her breathing shudders.

"Where are you now?" I charge toward the front of the shop and notice Jake just about to walk out of the door. Jake's attention falls on me, and my behavior has him on high alert.

"Grace and I have ourselves barricaded in the walk-in freezer. Blake, they cut power to the building," Ember states, and I instantly connect this information to the break-in at Kings Customs. There's no way it's a coincidence.

I lock eyes with Jake. "Someone is breaking into the bakery. Our women are hiding out in the freezer in total darkness." Jake says nothing as he pivots on his heel and bursts out the front door, damn near taking it off its hinges. "Ember, baby." I punch my fingertips against the control panel, setting the alarm, and follow Jake out the door. He takes off running down the sidewalk, leaving his ride since the bakery is only a block away. "Stay on the line." I switch the phone from one hand to the other and unholster my weapon, keeping it at my side. "We're on our way." I run to catch up with Jake.

"Hurry," Ember whispers, her teeth chattering from the cold room they've taken refuge in.

"I'm comin' for you, baby." I keep the phone to my ear, her breathing keeping me grounded as my heavy boots pound against the concrete on my way to her. Jake turns the corner, disappearing for a fraction of a second before I follow suit.

Jake already has his gun drawn, raised, and ready as we slow near the alleyway between the bakery and the adjacent building. He cautiously approaches the storefront, taking a glance inside. "No movement in the front of the store."

I peer around the corner, looking down the dark alleyway. Near the end, I see the bright red glow of taillights on what looks to be a dark vehicle parked around the back side of the bakery. "Prez." I keep my voice low, directing his attention to where I'm looking, and he takes note.

"You move in from the back while I enter through the front. I don't want these fuckers to have anywhere to run," Jake hisses, barely containing his rage. Separating from him, I silently move down the narrow alleyway, keeping my back against the brick. Within seconds of rounding the corner of the building, I lock eyes with a masked man in the driver-side mirror of a black car, and quickly shove my phone into my pocket, still keeping Ember on the line. At the same time, I hear gunfire echoing from inside the bakery. The fucker behind the wheel throws the vehicle in reverse. I fire a shot while plastering myself against the building to avoid getting struck. The driver's window shatters when I fire a second shot. The back tires screech, spinning against the asphalt as the man in the car drives forward. I pull the trigger again, the bullet shattering the back window. "Shit," I hiss, watching the fucker get away. With no time to waste, I shift my attention and rush inside, entering through the back door the thieves busted through.

"If you value breathin', I suggest you throw your fucking

weapon on the floor, step away from my man, and get on your motherfucking knees."

The warning voice I hear isn't Jake's. I slow my steps while making my way through the kitchen. My eyes fall on the walk-in freezer door to my right, and my heart hammers against my ribcage, knowing Ember and Grace are hiding inside it.

"Do it!" the unknown man shouts, clearly desperate and unhinged.

I move cautiously, and as quietly as possible in the direction the voice is coming from, which is near Grace's office.

"I guess we're both ready to die, 'cause I'm not droppin' my gun, you son of a bitch." The violent intent of Jake's tone leaves no misunderstanding that he is a man willing to die and take another life with him.

I ease toward the office. Standing in the doorway is the back side of a shadowy figure. "You'll be dead before your finger pulls that trigger," the guy says.

I silently step toward the man in a standoff with my brother and raise my weapon, pressing the barrel against the back of his head. "I doubt it," I growl. There's a beat of silence when no one says a word, and all I hear is this asshole's heavy breathing while he contemplates life. "Now drop your weapon before I put a bullet in your head."

As soon as I hear his weapon clatter on the floor, I pistol-whip the back of the motherfucker's head with enough force to knock his ass out. His knees buckle, and his body slumps to the floor.

"Get the women," Jake orders, and without hesitation, I rush back to the kitchen and pull open the freezer door. There, huddled in the back corner, with the glow of her cellphone shining on her beautiful face, is Ember with Grace at her side.

"Blake." Her eyes connect with mine, and she rushes me, throwing herself into my chest. I wrap my arms around her cold body.

I pull back, palming her face. "You two okay?" My thumb brushes against her chilled skin.

"Yeah. Cold, but we're okay." Ember takes a deep breath.

"Grace, baby." Jake walks into the freezer, brushing past me, and his woman enters his waiting embrace. "Jesus Christ." Jake bundles her into his side. "Let's get y'all out of here." He leads her out of the cold. I pull Ember into me and exit the freezer as well. "Grace, baby. You and Ember go upstairs to the apartment and wait until we come get you, understand?"

"Yes," Grace says softly, then she approaches Ember. "Come on."

Ember looks up at me as she pulls away and follows Grace toward the staircase to the apartment above the bakery.

"Help me toss these two motherfuckers in the freezer." Jake moves in the direction of Grace's office. The guy I knocked out still lies motionless in the doorway. Jake steps over him. "There's one more bastard I shot. He's behind the desk, out cold from me bashing the heel of my boot against his face. You take that one, and I'll grab this piece of shit."

Bending down, I put my hands under the prick's armpits and drag his heavy ass down the hall, through the kitchen. He moans as I toss his body onto the freezer floor. The man is soon accompanied by his accomplice, when Jake drops the man's limp body to the floor. "Look around for something to bind them with," Jake demands.

Using the light from my phone, I rummage through kitchen drawers, finding nothing before heading to the storage room in the back, where the exit is located. I finally find a couple of rolls of clear boxing tape. They will have to do, so I take them back to the freezer and quickly bind the men's hands behind their backs before wrapping tape around their ankles. As I walk out of the freezer and lock it from the outside, Jake is on his phone.

"We have a situation. Get a hold of Gabriel. Have him grab the van and come to the bakery. And tell him to grab Quinn on the way." Jake is silent for a beat. "Blake is on the scene with me. We'll wait here until Gabriel and Quinn arrive. I want all the other men at the clubhouse now," Jake barks, then ends the call.

Twenty minutes later, I'm standing just outside the back door, smoking, when lights flood the alleyway as a van with Gabriel behind the wheel drives toward me. I drop the cigarette at my feet and snub it out with the toe of my boot. Gabriel leaves the van running and steps out, and Quinn climbs out of the passenger side. Both make their way over.

"Where's Prez?" Gabriel questions.

"In the front of the store, keeping watch." Before I can say more, Jake appears.

"The pieces of shit are in the freezer. You two—" Jake motions to Gabriel and Quinn "—load 'em up. There's blood in the office. Get that shit cleaned before you leave. And do something with this busted door. I don't want the place left unsecured. Got it?" He keeps his eyes on both brothers, and they nod. "The rest of the mess; we'll take care of it later." Jake then faces me. "Ember rode with Grace. I need you to get her back to the clubhouse."

"You got it," I tell him.

"I'm taking my woman home. Nothing else happens until I get back to the clubhouse," Jake adds before walking back inside to get Grace.

Quinn pats Gabriel on the back. "Let's go fuck with some meat popsicles, big man."

Gabriel grunts, walking inside, and Quinn follows, lighting the way with a flashlight.

I stroll back into the building as Jake emerges from the staircase, bringing the women downstairs. "I need my bag." Ember walks over to where aprons are hung by hooks on the wall, retrieving her purse.

Reaching out, I take her by the hand and walk her outside, keeping her close to my side. I lead her toward the tattoo shop, which only takes a minute or two to reach, then I let go of her hand long enough to straddle my bike.

"Climb on." I look at Ember, waiting for her to slide in behind me. She's been on the back of a bike before, just never mine. Ember lifts her purse strap over her head, placing it across her chest before settling behind me. Her legs hug me as she shifts her body forward, her hands falling to my sides.

"This okay?" She brings her hands to rest on my stomach. The connection sends a bolt of energy through my body, much like having her body tucked in close to mine when she slips into bed beside me. Regaining my composure, I throw the bike into gear and drive away. I increase my speed the moment we hit the open road. Ember tightens her hold, her hands fisting my shirt while her breasts press firmly against my back as she leans in closer. I become torn between going faster to increase the intensity of our connection by making her hold on even tighter, or slowing down to prolong having her on the back of my bike. I would choose the latter if the club weren't already dealing with an urgent situation. Instead, I maintain my current speed to return to the clubhouse.

Too soon, the Kings' compound comes into view, and Grey is outside operating the gate. Approaching the clubhouse, I noticed Nikolai's bike and Demetri's SUV parked near the end of the building. By the front door, Demetri's right-hand man and driver, Victor, has his arms crossed over his chest. I pull up and back my ride alongside the other member's bikes. Ember slowly releases her hold on me, then dismounts and waits for me to join her before heading for the door.

"Hey, Victor," Ember greets our surprise visitor.

"Ember," he says, his face devoid of emotion.

"Victor." I extend my hand, shaking his. "Prez expecting y'all?"

"No," he says bluntly, but I take no offense. Victor is a man of few words, much like Gabriel.

"All right, man," I tell him, then Ember and I walk inside. I expected to find my brothers milling around the common area, but the place is empty. Raine walks out of the back room where we store extra booze, with a box in her arms.

Her attention goes to Ember. "Ember." She places the box on the bar and walks over. "I heard what happened. Are you okay? How's Grace?"

"A little shaken up now that the adrenaline of the situation is wearing off, but I'm fine, and so is Grace."

"Where is everyone?" I ask Raine, who then shifts her eyes from Ember to me.

"Oh, um. Logan ordered everyone to the shed."

I turn to face Ember. "Go fix yourself a bath. I'll come to check on you later."

Ember lets out an exhausted sigh, and I can tell she's beginning to feel the after-effects of tonight's event. "A bubble bath does sound nice."

My lips are pressed against her forehead before I think about my actions. Fuck. Why do I lose my damn senses whenever I'm near her? *Get your shit together, Blake.* She's fine. Nothing happened tonight. But something could have happened, and the weight of that thought alone is crushing me. I pull back and lock eyes with the woman I want but am convinced I do not deserve. Ember stares back at me with her doe eyes, lips parted ever so slightly. "Go," I say, swallowing the urge to kiss her.

Raine's eyes dart between Ember and me before she tugs Ember's arm. "Go get that bath started, and I'll whip you up one of my famous fried peanut butter and jelly sandwiches."

"Now you're speaking my language." Ember smiles at Raine.

With a final look my way, she walks away, and I head in the opposite direction, back outside.

The shed, which is a barn, is located on the back of the property. When I get there, I notice the van backed up to the barn doors and Gabriel dragging a bound man from inside. I walk inside to find all my brothers are present, along with two extra family members: Nikolai and Demetri, who've been out of town handling shit back in Russia.

Jake makes his presence known. "String these cocksuckers up."

Our guests are alert and fighting against my brothers' hold as they're led over to a chain with two large hooks, which hangs from a beam between two rafters. Gabriel cuts the box tape from one man's wrists to bind his hands in front of him again, using some thin metal cable. He then tosses the roll of cable to Logan, who repeats the process on the other man. Gabriel and Logan slip their bound wrists over the hooks, then Reid and Quinn work together, pulling the chain through the pulley wheel and hoisting the bastards off the ground, one back against the other's. The metal cords immediately begin tearing at the men's flesh under the weight of their bodies, causing one of them to growl in pain.

Jake rips their black ski masks off, revealing both men's faces, and the second one spits in Jake's face. Though warm outside, the air around us turns ice-cold, and Jake's lips thin with displeasure. Gabriel steps up, unsheathing a knife from his boot, and passes it to Jake. Logan walks over with rusty pliers and pries the fucker's mouth open. He thrusts the pliers into the man's mouth, clamping down on the piece of shit's meaty tongue. The guy struggles, biting into his tongue as Logan assists him in keeping it stuck outside his mouth. We all watch as our Prez reaches out and drags the blade across the motherfucker's tongue, cutting off the tip. He bellows as a torrent of blood flows from his mouth. "Shut the bastard up," Jake growls.

Reid comes over with a bandana and stuffs it into the injured man's mouth. Tears stream down the unlucky fool's face, and snot drips from his nose. Soon after, he passes out, his head flopping forward.

"Fuckin' weak-ass pussy," Quinn grumbles.

"You have no idea who the fuck you're messing with," the currently uninjured man warns.

"Well then, by all means, enlighten us as to whom we have the pleasure of entertaining." Jake steps in front of the man who spoke.

The ugly fuck sneers. "You'll find out soon enough, once word gets back to my club."

Club? So, these assholes are part of an MC?

"I saw no colors on your backs. That tells me you have no club, and the words spillin' from your mouth are lies," Jake says, his tone flat and unimpressed by the man's attempt to intimidate.

"I don't have to prove shit to you," the guy spews.

"You not only stole from my club once, but you've done it twice now. Whether word gets back to your club or not, you won't be breathin' to hear about it. However, I might be persuaded to quicken your deaths if given a little information." Jake begins circling the men. "What's the name of this club you speak of?"

"Fuck you. I'm no snitch," the man says.

"I admire your loyalty." Jake reaches into his cut, producing a cigar and lighting it. He looks over at Demetri, who's enjoying the show. "Appreciate the gift, brother. Welcome home." He takes a toke.

Demetri grins. "This is one hell of a reception, my friend."

Jake returns his attention to our guests. "You and your club stole a shit ton of money from us. More importantly, you endangered the lives of a couple of our women." Jake looks at me and jerks his head. "And I think that needs repentance, which my brother here is very eager to help you with."

I stroll over, glance at the table full of various devices we use to exact pain, and contemplate which tool I'd like to use first. I pick up a dirty blade, the handle of the knife wrapped in layers of silver duct tape. Once in front of the man running his mouth, I cut open his black shirt, exposing his hairy, heavily-tattooed chest. I look into his eyes while dragging the blade against his skin, making my first cut. He grits his teeth, stifling his scream. I make another cut, making my mark on him into an upside-down V before turning my back on him and replacing the knife in my hand with a pair of pliers. I grip his bleeding flesh at the peak of the V-shaped slash and pull down, peeling layers of skin from his body.

"Son of a bitch!" he screams and thrashes, which makes the wire around his wrists dig in a little deeper.

"Got something to tell us?" Jake asks.

The man groans, his body quivering from the pain. "Fuck. You." He emphasizes each word.

Jake looks at me again, and I walk over to the torture table, drop the pliers, and pick up a sledgehammer.

"I've got to give it to ya. You're tougher than your friend here." Jake stands before the guy who lost part of his tongue, holds his eyelid open, and puts his cigar against the fucker's eye. The blood-soaked bandana in his mouth muffles his scream.

Without delay, I swing the head of the sledgehammer down on the hanging man's kneecap, then repeat the process on his left just as fast. I begin thinking about what could have happened to Ember if we hadn't gotten there when we did. The thought of any man touching her fills me with a towering rage I've never felt before. Needing to release the anger, I drop the hammer to the ground and use the motherfucker as a human punching bag. I land one blow after another, burying my fist into his cut and scraping my knuckles against his teeth as I pummel his face. I keep going until I've spent all the energy inside my body. My fisted hands fall to my sides, and I take a few steps back. Sweat trickles down my face. I stare at the bloody body swaying before me, his face broken and contorted from the beating I just delivered. It's been a long time since I've done this much damage to someone. I'm not going to pretend that it doesn't feel good.

Gurgling noises start coming from the cocksucker, and Doc steps forward, inspecting the guy. He pries the man's eyes open. "Most likely brain damage." He looks back at Jake. "He's a goner. No good to us now." With a nod from Jake, Doc draws his gun, presses the end of the barrel against the man's temple, and pulls the trigger, ending his life permanently.

"Keep the other one alive. We'll revisit him later," Jake says. "Grey, help Blake dispose of the body. Let's wrap this shit up for the night. We all deserve a beer before returning to our families." Jake turns his attention to me, his hand clamping down on my shoulder. "You good?"

I stare down at my blood-stained hands, feeling empty. "Yeah."

"You did good tonight," Jake assures me, and I believe in his words as much as he does. He squeezes my shoulder and takes his leave.

Over the next hour and a half, Grey and I dig a grave for the dead man where several other unmarked graves stay hidden. No words are spoken as we roll the body into the deep hole, then begin shoveling earth onto his corpse.

Back at the clubhouse, while the others enjoy a beer, I head straight for my bedroom to wash what remains of the day from my body. I strip off my clothes, enter the shower, and turn on the cold water. I hiss at the icy spray against my hot skin, but it's a much-needed shock to my system. I watch blood, mixed with the soil from my arms and hands, swirl around the drain.

Once clean, I dress and head for Ember's room, again pausing outside her door. I twist the handle and step inside, where I find her lying on her side, fast asleep. I quietly close the door and cross the room. I grab a half-eaten sandwich from the nightstand, take a bite, and turn off the lamp. After finishing the sandwich, I slide between the sheets. I let my guard down and pull Ember's body against mine, because tonight I need to feel something other than emptiness.

"Blake," Ember whispers.

"Yeah?"

"I'm glad you're here."

Her words are a baptism, cleansing my soul of sin.

8

EMBER

Hearing my phone ping rapidly, I step out of the shower, then pad across the room to where it is lying on the bed. Picking it up, I smile when I see the barrage of texts from a group chat created by Glory.

Glory: Hey, bitches. I'm calling it a girl's night at the clubhouse. I'll be there in thirty with wine.

Grace: I'll bring cake.

Emerson: Beer.

Bella: Tequila!

Mila: I got the ice.

Leah: Charcuterie board.

Sofia: Pizza.

Me: Margarita mix.

Lisa: I was already in bed, but I'm getting up for this.

Raine: I'll have to take a raincheck.

Glory: Raincheck? What could be more important than girls' night?

Raine: I have a date.

Bella: Date?!

Mila: Date with who?

Glory: We need deets, Raine!

Raine: Calm your tits, girls. I have to get ready, but I promise to tell you later.

Bella: We won't forget.

Raine: Trust me, I know.

Glory: Emma, are you ignoring us?

Emma: I thought this chat was sent to me by mistake.

Emma came to us through New Hope House a couple of years ago. She had been in a bad situation but got her life back, thanks to Sofia. She has her apartment and a job working for the local library. She's still stand-offish and is most comfortable keeping to herself. The club and the women have taken her under their wing. Leave it to Glory to pull her out of her shell, though.

Glory: Seriously? You better have your ass ready by the time Victor pulls up.

Lelani: This is Austin. My woman is busy.

Glory: Busy? Yeah, we all know what that means. Lelani, your man is a party pooper.

I snort when Glory's following text comes through.

Glory: Alba, don't think you can escape girl's night. Tell that man of yours to let you up for some air. You can work on baby number four later.

A minute later, Alba replies.

Alba: Stooopp!

Glory: Victor is playing chauffeur tonight.

Shaking my head, I toss my phone on the bed, walk over to the dresser, and pull out a pair of cotton sleep shorts, a baggy tee, and my favorite pair of fuzzy thigh-high socks.

I'm not at all surprised Glory called a girls' night. After what happened yesterday, we could all use the distraction. To be honest, I've been freaking the hell out. The guys have been pretty tight-lipped, but, judging by their demeanor, some shit is about to hit the fan.

Victor picking the girls up and bringing them here was no doubt arranged by Demetri and Jake. The men won't be taking any chances regarding the safety of their women and family. Even Blake has been more alert since last night. Whenever I turn around, he's there, ensuring I'm good. Once Blake left my room, I had trouble sleeping. When I got up to get something to drink from the kitchen, he and Grey were sitting at the table talking in hushed tones, which ceased when I entered the room. Earlier, I overheard Blake on the phone with Jake telling him Grey was walking the perimeter outside, which they've done repeatedly throughout the day. And tonight, Jake made Raine agree to take one of Demetri's men along on her date, once he assured her he'd stay out of sight. All the extra activities and added security have me hyper-aware of my surroundings, but I know the Kings will take all measures to keep everyone safe.

Forty minutes later, I'm lounging on the sofa with my computer resting on my lap when the clubhouse door opens, and Glory walks in with Victor trailing behind. Behind them are Bella, Alba, Emerson, Mila, Sofia, Leah, Emma, and Lisa. I set my laptop on the table and jump up from the couch. "Hey!"

"Hey yourself," Glory greets back. "And I'm digging the hair, Ember."

I run my fingers through my rose-gold locks. My hair is not entirely bright pink but more blonde with a pink tint. "Thanks." I chuckle when I notice Glory's top reads *I need a cocktail. Hold the tail.* "Nice shirt." Glory has a thing for dirty humor.

Behind Glory, Victor mumbles under his breath—no doubt

giving her shit. Glory spins on her heels with her hand on her hip. "Hey. This is a girls' night. No boys allowed."

"Retract the claws," Victor grunts, then quickly makes himself scarce, like Grey and Blake did as soon as they got word girls' night was about to commence.

Over the next hour, we play catch-up on what everyone has been up to since Glory went out of the country with Demetri. Alba and Leah start talking about the bookstore, and they make sure not to skip over the part with me and the dipshit at the bank.

"So, Emma." Alba picks up her glass of wine. "How are things down at the library?"

Emma frowns. "Things are okay. However, it looks like I'll have to find a part-time job. They cut my hours again, and it's looking more and more like the rumors of the library closing their door may be true."

"Oh, Emma." Sofia jumps in. "I'm so sorry. I know how much you love working there. But I'll help you in any way I can."

Emma smiles. "Thanks, Sofia."

"Actually." Leah perks up. "Alba and I were talking and wanted to ask you something."

"Yeah?" Emma asks. "What is it?"

"Well, Alba and I are opening a bookstore."

Emma nods. "Of course. I'm so excited for you two. I can't wait to see it."

Leah continues, "We're so happy you feel that way, because Alba and I want to offer you a job. Full time, of course. If you like it there and things work out, we'd also love your help managing the place."

Emma sits stunned for a second. "Seriously?"

"Absolutely." Alba beams. "Leah and I will split our time there, but we need a manager. We couldn't think of anyone better suited for the job than you. Who else loves books as much as Leah and me?"

"I...I don't know what to say."

"We hope you'll say yes." Alba grins. "You'll be doing us a favor."

"Then I say yes," Emma agrees without hesitation. "A million times, yes."

From there, we keep the topics light while steering clear of the club's current drama.

"So, Ember." Glory takes a sip of wine, and I don't miss how all the girls have gone quiet.

I pause with a bite of cake halfway to my mouth. "What?"

"Anything new with you?" she asks.

"Nope. Nothing new here."

"Mmm hmm," Emerson hums.

"That's not what we hear," Mila mutters.

I cut my eyes to Alba and Leah, who are doing an excellent job of not looking at me.

"Yeah. Then what have you heard?"

"That you and Blake have something going on," Glory supplies.

I point my finger at the two gossiping culprits. "You two are the worst."

Leah ducks her head while Alba tries yet fails to look offended. "What! It's true. Besides, Grey is the one who said Blake leaves your bedroom early every morning, and he also says you've been playing your music almost every night for months."

"Sounds to me like Grey is more of a blabbermouth than my sister." Bella throws a cracker at Alba's head.

"Yeah, yeah, yeah. Grey's a blabbermouth, Alba's a blabbermouth. And we're all nosy as hell. Now spill the tea, Ember." Glory downs the rest of her wine and fills her glass again. All the other women are practically sitting on the edge of their seats, waiting for me to spill my guts. I blow out a breath and down a shot of tequila. "I have feelings for Blake."

"Well, no shit," Glory snips. "And the man is gone for you."

I shake my head. "It's not like that, and Blake doesn't feel that way about me."

Bella scoots closer to me on the couch. "Ember, the man sleeps in your room every night."

"Exactly. He sleeps. He comes in, lies on my bed, and I play for him until he falls asleep. Nothing more. Then he's gone by morning."

"You more than like him, don't you?" Grace asks.

I bite my bottom lip and let my silence speak for itself, because I don't dare to admit it out loud. Luckily, Sofia jumps in and steers the subject away from Blake.

"You know, I've heard you play before, and you play beautifully. When did you start?"

"I started playing the cello when I was six. I can play the piano and the flute, but I stopped practicing the piano and flute by the time I was fifteen. But I love the cello."

"What kind of parents make their six-year-old learn three instruments?" Alba questions.

"The kind with high expectations," I tell her. "Especially when they find out their daughter is gifted."

Mila pops a cube of cheese in her mouth. "Gifted?"

Sighing, I take a bite of cake. "I finished high school at age thirteen and graduated from college at eighteen with degrees in business and political science."

"Jesus Christ." Glory looks stunned. "How the hell did you end up here?"

"Glory!" Grace admonishes her best friend

"What? I didn't mean it like that." Glory looks back at me. "I'm sorry, Ember. I didn't mean it like that."

I laugh. "It's okay, Glory. I know what you meant, and I'm not offended. And I'm not ashamed of who I am or my role here. Trust me, I know what most people see when they look at me or find out what I do or have done for the club."

"Ember, I'm sorry. I honestly didn't mean..." Glory tries to explain.

"I know." I smile. "Nobody in this room has ever made me feel less-than. Never. And I'm grateful. The truth is, I love my life." I look at the women I consider my friends. "This club is my family. You all have accepted me from day one. This club has treated me better than the ones I share DNA with. With you and the guys, there are no expectations, no appearances to keep up, nobody demanding I be better and do better. I can just be me. Ya know?"

Emerson stands and walks over to sit by me. "I know first-hand what it's like to be weighed down by expectations. Though, I was lucky to have parents who eventually saw how toxic their behavior was and how it was driving a wedge into our relationship."

"Do you still see your parents?" Sofia asks. My heart breaks for Sofia, having lost her parents so tragically at a young age. "No." I shake my head. "Not for years. They disapprove of my lifestyle. I do have a relationship with my sister, though." I smile at the thought. "Scarlett is amazing. She's in college and is dating a mechanic."

"I bet your parents love that," Glory says sarcastically.

I laugh. "They don't know. She's been seeing him for a while. Keith is great, and he's good to my baby sister."

"What is she studying?" Grace asks.

I roll my eyes. "Political science, and she hates it. Dad wants her to become a lawyer, and he's basically pushing everything he'd hoped for me on Scarlett."

Mila huffs. "Why can't parents just let their kids be what they want? I'll never force my children to be anything but who they are." She looks at me. "Is your sister happy with what she's doing?"

"Hell no. She hates it. Scarlett has dyslexia. Every day at school is a struggle for her, but my parents ignore it. She wants to go to a fashion design school. I've been trying to convince her to move out here and let me send her to school, but she refuses. A part of me knows she wants to say yes. The problem is my little sister has a fear of disappointing our parents. That and they're good with the guilt trips."

"What do your parents do?" Bella asks.

I pick at the imaginary lint on my shirt. "My father just announced his run for Governor for the state of Georgia, and my mother is a homemaker slash southern belle society wife."

"Holy shit." Bella gapes.

"How did we not know all these things about you?" Alba asks.

Bella answers, "Because we're shit friends, that's how."

"No, you're not," I tell her. "I'm bad about keeping my personal life tight-lipped because it simply hurts too much to think about." I'm quiet for a second before adding, "But I'm learning it's nice to open up and share."

The room falls silent. Some women are smiling, and some are holding back tears.

"Damn, girl. I'd have brought more wine if I'd known we would get deep. I just wanted to know if you and Blake were doing the nasty and hoping for a few freaky sneaky details."

"Glory." I laugh. "You're crazy."

"I need another drink." Alba reaches for the margarita pitcher sitting beside my open laptop. I watch in horror as her eyes dart to the screen because my stupid self left it open. "Oh. My. God," she breathes.

I jump and slam the top closed on the laptop.

"What?" Bella asks.

"Oh my god," Alba says again.

"It's nothing," I nervously try to deflect.

Glory eyes me curiously. "What's nothing?"

I pick up my computer and hold it close to my chest. "Nothing."

"Oh, my freaking god," a stunned Alba repeats.

"Jesus Christ, Alba. Will you stop saying that and just tell us what's going on," Bella demands.

"There's nothing to tell," I try again.

"Hmm," Glory hums. "I think there is."

Alba grabs onto my arms with both hands. "You're Ellise Brooks?"

"What?!" Leah jumps.

A confused Mila asks, "Who is Ellise Brooks?"

Leah rushes me. "Shut up. Is it true?" Then she looks at Alba who then looks back at her. Together they say, "Oh my God!"

I close my eyes and count to five. This cannot be happening.

"Is anyone else lost?" Emerson chimes in.

There's a chorus of "yeah" from Glory, Sofia, Mila, Bella, and Grace. Alba ignores everyone. "Ember, how could you not tell us? This is huge." She turns to Leah, who is still staring at me dumbfounded.

"Stop looking at me like that." I bump her with my shoulder.

"Ellise Brooks."

I bite my bottom lip. "Look, it's not a big deal."

Alba snaps, "Not a big deal! Are you crazy? This is the biggest deal?"

"Alba, calm down."

She blinks at me. "Ember, I just found out you are Ellise Brooks, and you are telling ME to calm down?"

"Enough!" Glory throws her hands up. "Now I think I speak for the rest of us when I say, what the hell is going on and who the hell is Ellise Brooks?"

Alba side-eyes me and nods toward the six women who are currently looking very confused and very curious.

Sighing, I plop down on the couch, throw my head back and close my eyes to let out an exasperated sigh. "I'm Ellise Brooks."

"Come again? I thought your name was Ember?" Glory asks, still confused.

"It is. My full name is Bailey Ember Rhoads, but that's beside the point. My pen name is Ellise Brooks."

Sofia questions, "Pen name for what?" while Bella gasps and looks at Alba. Alba smiles and nods. Now I know Bella is not into books like her sister, but lord knows Alba has talked her ear off about the subject enough over the years for her to understand what we're talking about when we say pen name.

"I swear to all that is holy; if you bitches don't stop with all the weird lingo and knowing looks, I'm going to lose my shit," Glory huffs.

Alba looks over at me and bounces on her toes like a giddy child. "Can I tell them?"

I huff out a laugh. "By all means. Though I don't think it's a big deal."

"Whatever. It's a huge deal, and you know it." She waves me off and returns to our group, still awaiting answers.

"Ember is Ellise Brooks, a romance author. They're the *same person*!" Alba practically squeals.

Glory looks at me, then at Alba, then back to me. "Is this for real?"

I shrug. "Yeah."

"You're an author?"

I nod. "Yes."

"Not just any author," Leah breaks in. "Ember is a *USA TODAY* bestselling author."

The silence in the room is deafening, and everyone looks at me with stunned expressions.

Glory sets her glass down and stands. "Let me get this straight. You are a bestselling author?"

I bite my lip. "Yes."

"And you didn't think this was something your girls should know?" She throws her arms up.

"I mean..." I try thinking of a way to explain why I've kept this secret for as long as I have. "I planned on telling you all one day."

"Why not when you published your first book?" Grace asks. "Or when you were writing it?"

"Scared," I admit.

Bella cocks her head. "Scared of what?"

"Failing!" I cry. "My whole life, I've never really had a passion for anything. I used to think something was wrong with me, because I had no dreams of being a doctor, lawyer, or teacher. I didn't fit in. Then I came here, and the club accepted me. Nobody ever questioned what I was going to do with my life. I was able just to be me and be content. Then Alba and Leah invited me into their crazy book-obsessed circle."

"Hey," Alba grumbles.

I bump her shoulder. "But I'm forever grateful you did. Because I fell in love with reading. Then, one day, I started having thoughts and ideas and making up stories inside my head. The next thing I knew, I had completed my first manuscript." I look at my friends. "I didn't tell anyone because I didn't want you all to witness me failing if it should happen. To be honest, I didn't think I could do it."

"Ember." Leah walks over and wraps her arms around me. "I wish you would have said something. We're always in your corner, no matter what."

"I know that now. And I know I shouldn't have kept my secret for as long as I have. I never expected my books to blow up as they have."

"Damn." Glory plops back down on the couch. "Again—" she waves her hands "—I came here expecting her to admit she's knocking boots with Blake, and instead, she's ousted as a bestselling romance author."

Lisa lifts her glass in the air. "Best damn girls' night I've ever been to."

"I'll drink to that," Emerson agrees.

9

BLAKE

It's early, and the sunlight is just beginning to break through the shadows of the trees. I keep a steady speed while driving the UTV, following the fence line as Grey and I patrol the perimeter bordering the west side of the clubhouse's property. There's a ghostly gray mist crawling along the tall blades of grass. The lack of conversation between my brother and me gives me time to think, most of my thoughts swirling around Ember. My feelings for her are becoming difficult to keep at bay.

"What's eatin' you this mornin'?" Grey breaks the silence I've been soaking in.

"Nothin'," I mutter.

"Bullshit," he huffs. "We've known each other for a few years now, brother, and I consider you my best fuckin' friend, so don't go bullshittin' me. You've been more withdrawn than usual the past couple of days."

I roll my neck, feeling the tension build at the base of my skull. "Just dealin' with some shit."

"This shit you're speaking of happen to have rosy hair, gray eyes, and curves like a back country road?"

Grey mentioning Ember's curves has me white-knuckling the steering wheel. It's been a long time, but knowing my brother has been with Ember fucks with me sometimes. I mean; it shouldn't. When Grey realized I'd gone and caught feelings for Ember, he never touched her again. I grip the steering wheel tighter, reeling in that ugly green-eyed motherfucker. I have no right to feel this way. Hell, I've had my fair share of pussy, and I sure as shit don't have any claim on Ember's. Though I want to. I want nothing more than to mark her as mine.

"Y'all need to quit skirtin' around these feelings for one another. Stop fightin' it, brother." Grey hits hard with his words. I remain silent, but he continues. "You are nothin' like that sorry piece of shit," he says with bite. His words are nothing I haven't heard before from him or other brothers who know my story. "You can't keep clinging to his ghost, man. He's dead; his remains are nothing more than recycled worm shit. Don't let anything he said or did hold you back from being fuckin' happy."

I breathe, trying to absorb his words, knowing he's right but struggling to believe in myself enough to let them sink in.

After a few moments of silence hanging between us, the shed appears. Leaving our previous conversation behind, I bring the UTV to a stop. Following orders, Grey and I stroll over to the double doors, unlock the deadbolt, and remove the chain before pulling them open and walking inside. The air reeks of piss, and the pungent smell comes from the man in the middle of the barn.

"How long do you think Prez will keep him alive?" Grey walks over, checking the half-empty IV bag keeping our guest hydrated and alive.

"Fuck if I know. I'm surprised he hasn't put a bullet in the bastard already, since the cocksucker isn't talking."

The guy struggles to lift his head, so I fist a handful of his greasy hair and lift it for him. Crusty rust-colored blood covers his mouth and chin. The foul smell of his breath churns my stomach.

"He's breathin', for now." I release my hold on him, and his head flops back down. I grab a bottle of water and rinse my hand. "Let's head back. Church should be starting soon."

We leave, put the chains and lock in place, load up in the UTV, and head back toward the clubhouse.

The other men rolled in a short time later, and we're gathered around the table as Church begins. Jake starts us off. "Our guest still hangin' in there?" He looks between Grey and me.

"Still breathin'," I report.

"Prez, the fucker is starting to stink," Grey adds, scrunching his nose, remembering the stench.

"Nothing notable to hint at what club they claimed to be a part of. They had no IDs. And the one we're keeping alive isn't talkin'." Logan states the obvious, his frustration at the situation apparent.

"I vote we put a bullet in the bastard and move on," Quinn chimes in. "The claim that they belong to a club could be nothing more than a lie."

"Perhaps." Jake scrubs his beard. "However, we can't forget about the one that got away. There's a possibility he went runnin' back to someone, and that alone is cause for concern," he says and heads nod around the table at the truth Prez speaks. The unseen and unknown are more of a threat to the club. You can't defend yourself against what you can't see. Our leader sits silently for a few beats. "Gabriel, you and Blake get the pleasure of putting that worthless piece of shit out of his misery. For now, we remain alert. There's no immediate threat to the club, so keep going about everyday life with an extra awareness of what's happening in our town and who's coming through it. Eyes and ears, men. Got me?"

A round of "yeah" echoes off the walls, followed by Jake smacking the gavel against the table's surface. "All right, brothers. We got day jobs to get to." Jake's eyes land on Gabriel. "Let me know when the job is done."

"You got it, Prez," Gabriel mutters, then his indifferent stare finds mine. He says nothing, but I know he means for me to follow him out of the room, which is what I do. We stroll through the clubhouse. On the way, I make eye contact with Ember, sitting on one of the sofas, her legs crisscrossed, with a laptop. She smiles at me, and the gesture wraps around my heart like a warm embrace. Too soon, I take my attention from her beautiful face and walk out the front door. Gabriel heads across the yard to where the van is parked and climbs behind the wheel, and I jump into the passenger seat. He takes off, heading for the back of the property. I say nothing to him, knowing the mindset he has entered with what we're about to do.

Once inside the barn, where the soon-to-be dead man is strung up like a meat rack, Gabriel moves about until he finds a shovel. "Get him down." he orders, his tone filled with darkness. Following the order, I lower the man to the ground, then rip the needle from his arm. The guy moans, trying to move his arms, no doubt stiff and painful from being strung above his head for so long. The cable binding his wrists together is embedded in his skin. Gabriel walks outside, tosses the shovel into the van, then strolls back inside and squats, grabbing the broken bastard by his arms.

"Get his feet," he says, and working together, we carry the man out and chuck him inside the van. I slam the back doors closed and take shotgun, then Gabriel drives to the dumping grounds where we buried the other guy a few nights ago.

Once there, I take my pocket knife and cut through the layers of tape wrapped around the man's feet, then step back. "Out." I aim my gun at his face.

The piece of shit hesitates, but he finally swings his feet out of the back of the van. He's weak, but he stands. "Move," I order, and he slowly limps toward the freshly-turned dirt. Gabriel produces a pair of wire cutters and snips the binding around the guy's wrists. My brother then tosses the shovel at our thief's feet.

"Dig," he growls.

The man shakes his head in defiance.

Gabriel clenches his jaw. "Your other option is a slow death from dismemberment. Take your pick."

The man seems to reconcile with his impending death, and he picks up the shovel and begins digging his final resting place.

Several hours later, I'm reclined on the sofa inside the clubhouse, acting as a bystander while the brothers and their women enjoy a few drinks and listen to the music that fills the room, along with their banter.

Ember slides in beside me. "You've been sitting over here all by yourself most of the afternoon. Are you okay?"

"Got a lot on my mind."

Ember places her hand on my thigh, and my pent-up tension eases at her touch. "Anything you feel like talking about?"

"No." The truth is, I'm feeling drained, both physically and emotionally. I need to get away for a few hours and know where I want to go. "I'm out of here." I stand.

"Oh, um, okay," The disappointment in Ember's voice has my attention, and I look down at her. She's staring down at her lap, then she raises her head so her soul-searching eyes connect with mine.

"Come with me."

Ember cocks her head, and her eyes widen in disbelief. "Really?"

"Yeah."

She rises from the sofa and sweeps her palms down, fidgeting with her clothes. "Do I need to change?"

"You're perfect just the way you are." I reach out and take her hand, tugging her toward the direction of the front door.

"Wait; shouldn't I say something to Jake before leaving?"

Ember keeps pace with me as her eyes scan the room. Only then do I notice all the casual chatter around us has stopped, and all eyes have fallen on the two of us making our escape. I stride past the table that Jake, Logan, Austin, Quinn, and their women are occupying and pause. "Need us for anything?" I ask Jake, and his eyes dart between Ember and me.

"Nothin' comes to mind." He keeps a straight face, but the old lady beside him, Grace, doesn't attempt to hide the satisfied smile she's wearing. "Ride safe and keep the rubber side down, brother."

"Have her home by midnight, son," Quinn chimes in then lifts his beer. "And remember: love is cleaner with a packaged wiener." He winks at us.

"Quinn," Bella, Grace, Emerson, and Lelani chastise in unison.

"What?" He exaggerates being clueless.

With Ember at my side and all eyes in the room on us, I continue heading for the door. Behind our backs, Quinn adds with a fake emotional sniffle, "Our Blake is growing up. I'm so proud."

"Oh my God." Ember giggles slightly at Quinn's performance, and I can't help but chuckle. He is who he is, and is not ashamed to live authentically. I admire that about him. His humor holds no malice. It's simply the way he communicates with others to show he cares.

Once outside and away from the weight of everyone's stares, I turn to Ember after reaching my bike. "You change your mind?" she says quickly.

"Hell, no." I step into her space, filling the small gap between us. "You?"

"Where are we going?" She smiles, and like a magnet, she draws my face closer to hers. The smell of her floral perfume invades my senses.

"You'll see." I step back and swing my leg over the seat. With one glance from me, she smiles again, places her hand on my shoulder for balance, and slides in behind me. Just like the last time, her hands wrap around my middle. Not waiting for another beat, I fire up the engine and pull away from the clubhouse.

The farther my bike carries us down the highway, the lighter I become. Nothing compares to the unbridled freedom of the sun on your face and the wind kissing your skin while on the back of a Harley. I look in my side mirror and catch Ember with her eyes closed and the wind whipping through her hair. Does she have any idea what she does to me? I put my eyes back on the road and increase my speed, making Ember's hold on me tighten, and the smile on her face grows. I lean back, dropping my arm, and wrap my hand around Ember's calf. The simple gesture holds more meaning, and judging by the way Ember slides in closer and presses her chest flush against my back, she understands what I'm feeling without saying anything. She lays her head between my shoulder blades, and one of her palms slides up my torso, resting on my chest. I wonder if she feels my heart beating like a jackhammer. At this moment, I know without question that I want her on the back of my bike for the rest of my life. I wonder if she feels the same.

A short while later, I turn on a side road and follow it for a few miles until we come to a fork, then take a left turn onto a dirt track, which is also the start of my property. After cresting the hill, the barn comes into view. A few minutes later, I'm bringing the bike to a stop. Ember climbs off first, and I'm quick to follow.

"So this is where you disappear all the time." She takes in the rolling fields of waving grass and wildflowers. "Look at that." She points toward the body of water, visible over the treetops in the distance. "You can see the lake from here."

I slide open the barn door. "You can see it better from the loft." I grab her by the hand and lead her inside.

"Wait." Ember stops in front of an unfinished sculpture. She runs her fingers along the rough edges that have yet to be smoothed out, tracing the shape of a woman's body and the cello between her legs. "Blake," she whispers, "is this... me?"

"We're going to miss it." I pull her away.

"Miss what?"

I point to the ladder leading to the loft overhead. "Go on up, and I'm right behind you."

She places a foot on the bottom rung, then reaches above her head and starts to climb. After she has gotten up the ladder, I climb up behind her. Once at the top, I direct her to sit on a futon. "Have a seat." I scrub my palms down the front of my jeans and step away for a second to pull the cord on an old vintage floor lamp with one of those fringe bottom shades, bathing the dark loft in warm amber light.

"How do you have power out here? I don't remember seeing an electric pole."

Tucked away in the corner is a mini fridge, and I stroll over to grab a couple of chilled beers from inside. I pop off the tops using a bottle opener tied to a string hanging from the nearby wall, then I point above my head at the rafters and answer her question. "I installed a couple of small solar panels, and not having trees shrouding the place has advantages." I hand her the two bottles of beer and turn to unlatch the loft door, then pull it open.

Ember gazes at the perfect view of the setting sun reflecting on the lake. "Wow."

I sit beside her and she passes me a beer, which I lift to my lips, not once taking my eyes off her. The red glow seems to set her hair on fire and showcases the spattering of light brown freckles on the bridge of her nose, where the summer sun has kissed her skin.

"You're missing something wonderful here by staring at me." Ember's lips lift in a smile before she sips her drink.

"I'd rather look at you." I don't hold back the thought in my head.

That adorable dimple appears as her smile grows, but she keeps her attention on the Montana sky.

I finally turn my face toward the sun, watching as it dips below the horizon. Beyond the treetops, the light fans over the water, reflecting the dusky sunset sky's blood red, tangerine orange, and misty purple hues.

"I like you, Blake." Ember shatters the serenity that had encapsulated us.

I down the last of my beer before confirming what she has known for a while. "I like you too," I admit, though my feelings run deeper.

"Then what are we doing?" She keeps gazing at the now-deepening blue and charcoal horizon, watching dusk fade into twilight. "Why are you so hesitant to make a move or tell me how you feel?"

I swallow the proverbial lump of emotion stuck in my throat.

Ember shifts her body and faces me. "Is it because I'm a club girl?" There's a hint of insecurity in her voice I've never heard before.

"No." I squash whatever doubts she has about her role in the club. "Don't you ever think you aren't good enough for me or anyone else because you are part of the Kings family. You are more than worthy of any man you want."

"But I want you." Ember's confession races past her lips, and her mouth gapes open. She looks shocked at her words.

I stand abruptly and throw my empty bottle into the darkness outside the loft door. I reach my hands above my head and grip the wood frame of the opening. Hanging my head, I breathe in deeply. "I'm damaged goods, babe. I don't deserve you."

Ember is soon standing beside me, leaning against the door frame. "Is that what you think? That you aren't good enough for me?"

"I'm not worth loving, Ember." I say the words with a belief I've held onto for a long time.

Ember reaches out, her palm touching my cheek. "Says who?" she asks, and I can't answer. "Look at me, Blake."

I turn my body to face her and take one step closer.

"Was it your father? Did he tell you that?"

I can't do anything but stare into her eyes, but it's all she needs to know the answers to her questions.

"I don't know much, other than your father was not a good man, Blake. But I know enough about you to confidently say you are not your father, and you deserve love. You deserve to be happy. The biggest *fuck you* you can give him is by letting go of the control he still has over you."

I close my eyes while a battle ensues between my head and my heart. My heart thunders against my ribcage, my lungs tighten, and I feel like I'm fighting to breathe.

Ember's palm slides from my face, only to fist my cut in her hand. I soon sense her lips a breath from mine. "Let me love you, Blake."

Her words are my undoing. I crash my mouth down on hers. Her mouth just as hungry as mine, Ember moans. There's nothing sweet about our first kiss. It's an inferno spreading like wildfire. I slip my hand into her hair, gripping her neck as I draw her in more, bringing her body flush against mine. I slide my free hand down the curve of her waist and over the flare of her hip before palming her ass and lifting her off the ground. She squeezes her thighs against my hip, and her arms drape over my shoulders around my neck as I shift us away from the open loft door. When I push her back against the wall, she rolls her hips, rubbing against my cock, which is already pressed painfully against my jeans. I growl into her mouth and grind against her.

"Blake," Ember breathes.

My mouth leaves hers, trailing down the soft slope of her neck and her racing heart beating against my lips. I coax her feet to the floor, press my thigh between her legs, and widen her stance. I slide the thin strap of her shirt over her shoulder, exposing her breast. My mouth presses against hers once more as I roll her taut nipple between my fingers. "Please," Ember begs.

"You need more, baby?" I breathe.

"Yes," she says with a soft moan, and who am I to say no?

I unbutton her shorts, slowly drag down the zipper, and then slip my hand beneath the waistband of her cut-off jeans. "Fuck," I hiss, finding her pussy soaked and her clit swollen. I rub circles against her bundle of nerves, causing Ember to buck her hips. I drag my fingertips through her slick slit, then dip them inside her tight heat. She rocks her hips as I press the heel of my palm against her clit. "You're mine, Ember." I match her thrusting rhythm. Her legs start quivering, and her breathing quickens as she gets off. "That's it, baby. Give it to me." In seconds, her pussy tightens around my fingers as her orgasm shreds through her body.

Ember holds onto me as she recovers. I slip my hand out from her shorts and fasten them up, then I rest my forehead against hers as her breathing levels out. Her arms drop from around my neck, her hands falling between us, her fingertips fumbling to undo the button on my jeans.

I reach down, covering her hands with mine. "Stop."

"Blake, let me..." Her head lifts, and her eyes connect with mine.

"I want you, baby. More than anything I have ever wanted in my fuckin' life. But I want to take my time. I need you in my bed to map out every inch of your body before I fuck you."

Ember traces my bottom lip with hers, her breath mingling with mine. "Then what are you waiting for? Take me home."

· · ·

After what felt like the longest, most sexually charged ride of my life, Ember and I arrive at the clubhouse. Everyone who was here earlier is now gone except for Raine and Grey, who are the only ones sitting at the bar. "Hey guys." Raine smiles, and Ember gives her a slight wave. On a mission, I don't speak but hold tight to Ember's hand, blowing past their burning stares as we make our way to the stairs. "Goodnight," Raine sing-songs.

"About damn time," I hear Grey mutter once Ember and I reach the stairs' top.

Before we're fully in my bedroom, my mouth tastes Ember's once more. I peel her tank top over her head. Braless, her breasts sway as I dip my head, taking one of her nipples into my mouth. I growl at her responsiveness to my touch and switch sides, showing the other equal attention. I walk her backward toward the bed. Stepping back, I watch her shimmy out of her cut-off jeans and panties.

Ember stands bare before me; I can only stare, admiring every detail under the silver glow of moonlight shining through the nearby window. There's a vulnerability in her eyes I've not seen before.

I shrug off my cut, letting it fall to the floor, then peel off my shirt. I watch Ember keep her eyes locked on mine while cupping her breasts in her hands, rolling her nipples between her fingertips. Then, slowly, she drags her palms down over her flat stomach, one hand dipping between her thighs. "Blake, I'm going to combust if you don't touch me."

I'm hypnotized, watching her fingers caress her clit.

Suddenly, there's a sharp banging on my bedroom door. "Blake!" Grey shouts from the other side. He pounds his fist against the door again after no response. "Shit, man. I'm sorry, brother, but you need to get out here."

I growl in frustration, and Ember sighs, her hands falling to her sides. I close the gap between us. "This isn't over." Then I reach around her, pull the blanket off my bed, and wrap it around her naked body. With a quick press of my lips hard against hers, I say, "Give me a minute."

"I'm not going anywhere."

Turning, I cross the room and angrily swing open the door. "Someone better be dying, brother."

"We have company."

"Who?" I wait for him to elaborate.

"A young girl. She was lingering outside the compound gate and said she's looking for you."

The fuck?

I look back over my shoulder at Ember. "Go. I'll meet you downstairs," she says.

I leave the bedroom and follow Grey downstairs to find a willowy young woman with dark brown hair and large, light green eyes. They track my every move as I make my way around tables and chairs and approach her. Her pale skin against her black attire gives her a haunting appearance.

"Blake?" Her voice is a little shaky.

"Who's askin'?" My tone is a bit harsh, and it causes her to shrink back.

"My name's Bellamy," she states, swallowing hard. "I'm your sister—I mean half-sister. That is, my dad is your dad, but we have different moms." She fumbles over her words, but I'm still stuck on the *I'm your sister* part.

"I didn't know you had a sister, brother," Grey says.

"It's news to me." I keep staring at the young green-eyed girl.

Bellamy laughs nervously and twirls her long hair around one of her fingers. "Yeah, I just found out recently myself. Afterward, I got on a bus, and here I am." She sways a bit.

"You all right?" I question.

"Yeah. My sugar is probably low."

Her sugar? "Bellamy, are you a diabetic?" I ask, and she nods.

"Do you take pills or a shot?" I shift into a different mindset. My grandmother had diabetes, and I had to give her a shot of insulin a few times when she was too weak and shaky to do it herself.

"I take an injection."

"I assume you didn't hop on a bus and travel without it."

"I'm not stupid." She sighs, adding, "But someone on the bus stole my backpack, where I had my medication."

"She doesn't look so hot, brother." Grey looks on with concern.

Bellamy sways again. "Shit." I move into action and scoop her tiny body into my arms.

"I'm fine, just a little lightheaded."

"You're not fine," I tell her. "We need to get you something to eat." I then direct my attention to Grey. "Call Doc, and let him know what's going on and to bring appropriate medication."

"On it." Grey pulls out his phone.

"Blake." Ember calls my name, descending the stairs, and her eyes fall on the young girl in my arms.

"I'll explain in a minute," I say, noticing the questions brewing in her beautiful eyes. "Do we have any orange juice or soda?"

"Yeah."

"Grab some and bring it to me." I carry Bellamy over to one of the sofas and sit her down. Ember is back within seconds, holding a glass of orange juice and a can of soda. I take the juice and hand it to Bellamy, who steadily drinks until it's gone.

"Way to make a first impression," Bellamy mumbles, then raises her head to look at me. "I shouldn't be here." Then her eyes cut to Ember, who is standing beside me. "Hi."

Introductions are in order, even though Bellamy is still a complete stranger herself, though she claims to be my sister. "Ember, this is Bellamy." I pause for a beat. "My sister."

Ember looks at me, searching my eyes and knowing the storm already brewing in my head. She looks at Bellamy and smiles, then sits on the sofa beside her. "It's nice to meet you."

"Sorry about all the fuss." Bellamy smiles at Ember. "Thanks for the juice. I'm already starting to feel a little better."

Just then, Doc charges through the door with momma bear Lisa at his side. "So, I hear we let our sugar get too low." Doc drags a chair from the nearby table and sits before Bellamy. He digs into his bag and pulls out a glucose monitor. "Let's check your level and get the rest of your vitals. Then you can tell me which medicine you are currently on and the dosage." His kind eyes instantly put Bellamy at ease, and she holds out her finger for Doc to prick and get a blood sample.

For fifteen minutes or so, Doc cares for Bellamy. "She needs to rest," he tells me, after packing his things.

"Ember," I call, catching her attention, and she locks eyes with me. "Get Bellamy settled in my room for the night."

Ember turns to Bellamy. "Come on. I'll take you upstairs."

"I don't have anything to sleep in besides what I have on. All I had was in my bag," Bellamy says, sounding exhausted.

"That's okay. I'm sure I have something you can borrow."

Bellamy stands. "Blake."

"Yeah?"

"You may not be too excited at my existence, but finding out I have a brother is the best thing to ever happen to me."

Her words hit me harder than I expect them to. The truth is, I don't know how I feel at the moment, and I've had zero time to process anything since her arrival. For now, I'm left with more questions than I have answers. "The girls will make sure you're comfortable. We can talk tomorrow."

With no more to be said for the night, Ember and Raine take Bellamy upstairs.

"You alright?" Doc asks.

I let out a heavy sigh and run my fingers through my hair. A lot has happened in the past few hours, and I feel stuck on an endless rollercoaster ride.

"I'm sure you'll get the answers you're lookin' for come tomorrow. For now, try and get some shut-eye." Doc clamps his hand on my shoulder. "So that you know, Jake is already aware of the situation."

I nod. Good. One less thing for me to deal with tonight. "Thanks."

"If you need anything, don't hesitate callin' me back here," Doc says, then spots his woman across the room. "Come on, Lisa, baby. Let's go home."

A few hours later, the clubhouse is locked, and everyone has settled for the night. My back aches as I lie stretched out on a cot in the basement. I haven't slept in here for quite some time. Not since I was prospecting, anyway. The corners of the room are dark, with only a small amount of dim light coming from a bare bulb hanging from the ceiling with a pull string. Across the room sits a washing machine and dryer. Above them is a shelf holding a large bottle of laundry soap and fabric softener. I breathe in deeply. It still smells the same, a bit musty, mixed with the scent of clean laundry.

I close my eyes, willing my body to relax long enough to fall asleep, but I can't turn off the rampant thoughts keeping me awake. The cot squeaks as I get to my feet. There's only one person who has the power to silence the noise.

10

EMBER

I roll over in bed and look at the time. It's a few minutes past two in the morning, and sleep still evades me. I can't stop worrying about Blake and what kind of headspace he's in. Having a sister he didn't know existed show up tonight has sent him into a tailspin. Thank God she got to the clubhouse when she did. Now I'm left with more questions than answers regarding Blake. For as long as I've known him, he's been a closed book. He has never divulged where he came from, who his parents are, or given clues about his past. The only time Blake lets parts of his past rise to the surface of the abyss he is drowning in is when I play for him. For that split second, when our eyes connect and the music wraps him in its embrace, I see the pain scratching at the surface. But as quickly as it appears, it fades. Now, I can't help but worry about what danger lies ahead for Blake, especially with whatever situation brought this young girl to our doorstep.

I lie awake, waiting for Blake to walk through my door. I've spent many nights doing the same. Something has to give. I should go to him. I may need to make the first move for once. Sitting up, I climb out of bed, pad over to the chair in front of the window, and slip on the silk robe flung over the arm. Turning on my heel, I head for the door, but I pause the moment I go to turn the handle. *What if this is a bad idea?*

Lowering my hand, I begin to pace the length of my bedroom. "Leave him be, Ember. Forcing it could push him further away." I try to talk myself out of going to him. What if I push him, and it screws up what we have already? I stop pacing and look at my closed door. "Fuck it." I run to the door and fling it open, gasping when I run straight into Blake, whose large frame fills the doorway. "Blake," I breathe. "I was just about..." He cuts me off by crashing his mouth down on mine. I don't hesitate to grant his tongue access. He doesn't waste any time, either. He ushers us back, kicking the door shut with his booted foot while reaching between us and releasing the tie to my robe. His palms start at my shoulders and leave a trail of goosebumps in their wake as he slips the silk from my body. His hands never leave my skin as they trek down the sides of my breasts, his thumbs brushing over my hardened nipples pushing against my tank's fabric. I moan into his mouth when his large hands grip my ass and I'm lifted off my feet. I wrap my legs around his waist, and the friction of his jeans rubs against my panty-covered clit, causing me to gasp. "Blake."

A second later, my back is against the wall. "I'm done," he rasps, tugging down the front of my top, exposing my breasts.

"Done what?" I pant.

"Done fighting," he growls, just before dipping his head and taking my nipple into his mouth.

"Oh, God." My nails dig into his scalp, urging him to continue his assault. "More. I need more."

Black releases my nipple. "Fuck."

"Don't stop," I plead.

"Not a chance." He carries me over to the bed and sets me on my feet. From there, it's a frenzy to rid each other of our clothes. I pull Blake's shirt over his head while he kicks off his boots. Next, he frees me of my top. "Turn around," he orders.

Doing as I'm told, I slowly turn. Then I notice our reflections in the mirror mounted on my dresser across from the bed. "First, I'm going to fuck you, and you will watch as I make your pussy come all over my cock." Blake bites the column of my neck. "Then it's going to be my turn to watch as I lay you on your back, crawl between your thighs, and make love to you, Vita Mia."

I bite my bottom lip and rub my thighs together to try and alleviate the ache his words have caused. Behind me, Blake pulls the thin material covering my pussy from my body. "Be a good girl, Ember, and watch." A shiver wracks my body at his command, and I nod. In my euphoric haze, I miss the moment Blake strips out of his jeans, but I don't miss the velvety feel of his hard cock against my ass.

With one palm pressed against my back, Blake pushes me forward until my hands are flat against the bed. He takes his other hand and wraps it around the front of my neck, gently urging me to arch my back. His palm then trails its way down my back and over my ass until his fingers come into contact with my center.

"So fuckin' wet for me." He swirls his thumb over my swollen clit. "Put one leg up on the bed and spread." His grip on my neck tightens as I feel the blunt head of his cock kiss the entrance of my pussy. When he pauses, we make eye contact through the mirror. When our eyes meet, he drives forward, and I scream his name. *"Blake!"* It's as if time slows and the room fills with an electric charge. My skin prickles with an awareness that I know he, too, can sense. Blake's grip tightens around my neck. "You feel that? You feel me?" he grunts between thrusts.

"Yes," I breathe. "I feel you. Don't stop."

Soon, I start rocking backward, meeting him thrust for thrust. Sweat drips down between my breasts, and my fists clench the sheets. Out of nowhere, my orgasm starts to build. I don't want this connection between Blake and me to end, and I try to slow down our momentum.

"No," Blake growls, and suddenly I find my body lifted and my back flush against his chest. "You." *Thrust.* "Are." *Thrust.* "Going." *Thrust.* "To." *Thrust.* "Come."

I dig my nails into his forearm that's braced across my chest and give into what is already a losing battle.

"Now," he commands.

As soon as the word leaves his mouth, my pussy clamps around him, and I scream.

"That's it," he rasps against my ear. "Let me feel you flood my cock with that tight pussy."

My orgasm goes on for what feels like forever before my body goes lax in Blake's arms. When he pulls away, I hum at the loss of his heat.

"My turn now, Vita Mia." Blake lays me on my back, and the cool sheets feel good on my heated skin. And true to his word, he settles his large frame between my thighs, takes his heavy cock in his hand, and fills me again. I gasp when his cock stretches my tender pussy but welcome the mixture of pain with pleasure. True to his earlier words, Blake makes love to me soft and slow. And not once does he take his eyes off mine as he takes me over the edge before finally letting himself fall.

Hours later, the sunlight peeking through the window in my room wakes me, but I don't open my eyes. I don't want to open them and discover that what happened with Blake was a dream. Though, the ache between my thighs tells me I wasn't dreaming. I don't want to face the looming possibility that when I look over, the bed beside me will be empty and the sheets cold, just like so many mornings before. I can't bear the thought that last night wasn't as special to Blake as it was to me. Or that last night was just a way for him to escape. That last night he only saw me as a club girl. My heart tells me Blake would not use me...my body...in such a way, though. How he looked at me and held me as we made love says I'm not just a club girl. It says I'm his girl. And only his.

Opening my eyes, I sneak a glance, then swallow down a sob that threatens to escape. Blake lies beside me, looking more peaceful than I've ever seen. I keep perfectly still as I take the opportunity to absorb this moment into a memory. It's nice seeing Blake like this. He's always so tense and serious. But now, the lines on his face are relaxed, and he looks peaceful. I let my gaze travel south across the light dusting of hair on his chest as I admire the beautiful rose tattoo he has across his left rib cage. The rose is red, and in place of the stem is written in script, *I am, because you were,* and close to it more script that reads, *Grief is love with no place to go.* Though it's not visible to me now, I know his club piece covers almost his entire back.

The smell of coffee and bacon assaults my senses. The thought of bringing Blake breakfast in bed makes me smile. Careful not to wake him, I quietly ease out of bed and go to the dresser for shorts and a t-shirt before heading for the bathroom to take care of business. Relieved to see Blake still sound asleep, I exit the bedroom.

"Good morning." Lisa beams when I walk into the kitchen. "You're just in time," she tells me.

"Need any help?" I ask, pouring myself a cup of coffee and an extra to take to Blake.

Lisa takes a plate full of eggs, bacon, and toast to Doc, sitting at the table with Grey. "Nope. I got it covered. Why don't you sit down and eat with us?"

I panic and start thinking about how to leave with two plates of food and two cups of coffee without drawing questions. That's not something I thought of when I came to get Blake breakfast in bed.

Suddenly the thought of him wanting to keep things between us a secret fills me with dread.

"You okay, honey?" Lisa asks, bringing me out of my inner turmoil.

I peer over my shoulder to see a look of concern on her face. "Yeah, yeah. I'm good." I go about fixing my coffee.

"Mornin'." Blake's sleep-filled rumble fills the room, and I stop breathing.

"Morning, Blake," Lisa's cheery voice greets. "You hungry?"

"Starved," he tells her.

My hands begin to shake, and I feel like my heart will beat out of my chest. How do I act? What should I say? *Play it cool, Ember.* I give myself an inner pep talk. But that pep talk flies right out the window when Blake walks up behind me, wraps his arms around my waist, and kisses my neck. "Mornin', Vita Mia."

"Morning," I squeeze out.

"You get coffee, and I'll get the food, baby."

Unable to trust my voice, I nod.

Behind me, I hear Lisa comment, "How wonderful."

I turn on shaky legs to see Blake holding two plates piled with food, looking relaxed like what just transpired is a regular, everyday occurrence. Meanwhile, Lisa looks at the two of us like she could burst into tears any moment.

I sit beside Blake, who has already begun stuffing his face. Under the table, a foot kicks my shin. I look up from my plate to see Lisa giving me the goofiest grin, and I lift my mug to my lips to hide my smile.

Luckily, the awkwardness is broken when Grey speaks. "Talked to Prez this mornin', and he should be rollin' up any minute."

I turn to Blake. "How is Bellamy? I should go check on her." I scoot my chair, but a hand on my legs halts me.

"I looked at her when I got up. She's still asleep."

"Sleep is good, but she'll need to eat soon," Doc says, looking down at his watch. "I also talked to Emerson last night; she'll be over this morning to check over the girl."

"Appreciate ya, brother."

"I'll take her some breakfast when Jake gets here," I offer.

He squeezes my thigh. "Thanks, baby."

Just then, Jake walks into the kitchen. He stops, and I watch his eyes ping between us, Blake's hand on my thigh and my body turned into his. A ghost of a smile touches Jake's lips before it's gone.

Blake downs what's left of his coffee and stands. "I need to take care of a few things before the rest of the men arrive. Check on Bellamy for me?"

"I'll make sure she's taken care of."

Fifteen minutes later, I knock on Blake's bedroom door before opening it. I smile, seeing Bellamy sitting up in bed, rubbing at her eyes. "Morning, sweetie."

She blinks away her sleepiness and gives me a shy smile. "Hi."

"I thought you might be hungry." I hold up the plate. "Lisa made some eggs, bacon, and toast. I got you a bottle of orange juice too. I hope that's okay. If you don't like eggs and bacon, I can make you something else." I walk over and sit on the edge of the bed. Bellamy takes the plate from me and immediately starts digging in. "I love eggs," Bellamy says, taking a bite of bacon.

"I can see that." I giggle. "So, how did you sleep? I know how weird it can be in a strange place."

"I slept great. Better than I have in a long time." Bellamy sets her toast down and twists the cap off the bottle of juice. She takes a sip and looks unsure of what to say next.

"Look, honey, I know you don't know us, and being here might seem a little scary, especially with all the big burly men you'll meet soon, but you are safe here. Nobody will hurt you. Your brother is a good man, one of the best men I know."

Bellamy folds into herself, wrapping her arms around her middle. "I feel safe here. I don't know my brother, but he wouldn't hurt me." She looks away. "I know what bad is." She looks back at me. "Blake's not bad."

I swallow past the lump in my throat at Bellamy's admission. I see it in her eyes; this sweet young girl is no stranger to evil.

Plastering on a forced smile, I steer the conversation differently, hoping to change our moods. "How about you finish up your breakfast, then we can go into my room and raid my closet for something to wear? I don't have your exact size, but I'm sure we'll find something."

Bellamy perks up and smiles. "Okay."

11

BLAKE

The back of the clubhouse comes into view as I finish riding the perimeter of the compound and notice Bella, Alba, and Emerson outside, watching the kids play while drinking coffee. It's no different from any other day, at least not for them. My attention shifts to my second-floor bedroom window, where Bellamy is, hopefully, comforted by Ember. "I have a little sister." That's crazy to say out loud. Until now, I thought no one else alive shared my DNA besides my uncle, my father's brother. Thinking about him makes my blood run cold. My father was a shitty human but a fucking saint compared to his brother. Evil isn't a strong enough word for a man like him.

Parking the UTV, I walk into the clubhouse and find my brothers gathered inside, milling about, some with mugs of coffee and others holding plates of food, chowing down on the grub Lisa prepared early this morning.

I walk over to Jake, who is standing with Logan. "All clear?" Jake asks.

"Nothing to report," I'm quick to reply while scanning the room, searching for Ember and Bellamy.

Jake glances behind him, and I focus on Ember descending the stairs with my sister tucked into her side. The room falls silent as they approach.

I look at Bellamy, who, despite where she is, appears to be composed. "How are you feelin' this morning?"

Bellamy focuses only on me. "Better than last night." Only then does she glance between me, Jake, and Logan.

"Bellamy, this is the club's President, Jake, and Vice President, Logan." I introduce her to my brothers. She stands there, silent, shrinking to the size of a mouse. "I promise you're safe here." Why is she spooked?

"I'm not allowed to speak to any club member unless spoken to," Bellamy whispers, looking past me at Jake, whose expression turns cold.

Our President gives his undivided attention to my sister, his expression softening. "Sweetheart, I don't know who put the fear in your eyes that I'm seeing right now, but I promise you this club won't harm you. And if you've got somethin' to say, respectfully, then you are allowed to speak it freely," he assures her with nothing but kindness in his eyes. "You understand?"

She gives him a half smile, nodding. "I understand."

"Good." Jake then draws in a deep breath before announcing, "Church. Now."

"You okay?" I ask Bellamy.

Without warning, she throws herself into me, her arms wrapping around my waist. "Yeah."

My arms go around her shoulders, embracing her back. "Glad you're here, kid."

My sister leans her head back and looks at me. "Me too." Tears pool in her eyes.

Bellamy steps back, and my eyes connect with Ember's. "Come here." I pull her closer until I have her chest pressed against mine. "Thank you."

"For?" Ember raises her brow.

"Everything." My lips gravitate toward hers.

"Everyone is staring at us," she whispers.

"Let them. You're mine." I cover her mouth with mine in a bruising kiss for everyone to witness.

Shortly, I leave Bellamy and Ember standing in the middle of the room while I join my brothers, and we file into Church, where everyone takes their seats.

All eyes fall on me as I close the door and join my brothers at the table. Jake clears his throat. "You claimin' her?"

"Ember is mine. She's always been mine," I state.

"About fuckin' time!" Logan exclaims, leading to my brothers pounding their fists against the table's surface in agreement.

"All right," Jake's voice booms. "Let's get down to business." At his order, the room falls silent once more. "Any leads on our unwelcome guest who is now becoming compost as we speak?"

"Nothing," Reid reports. "The only evidence we obtained was camera footage of their getaway vehicle runnin' a red light on the night of the robbery at the bakery, which you're aware of."

"None of our street informants noticed any unfamiliar people in town recently," Austin adds.

Jake blows out a breath. "I don't like not knowing who those fuckers belonged to."

"Maybe they were lying about a club. Fear can make a man say anything." Quinn drums his fingers against the table.

Logan strokes his beard. "No. They never broke. Like it or not, the bastards are loyal to someone. We can chalk up not wearin' colors to hiding their connection to a club. No matter how cowardly we think it is, it's a strategic move that keeps criminal activities from being traced back to others."

"Agree." Jake nods. "And the fucker who got away no doubt headed back to where he came from, leaving us looking behind our backs, waiting for shit to hit the fan. And, for once in our lives, we have no goddamn idea which direction we should focus on." His brows draw together, making the crease between his eyes more prominent. Prez releases a frustrated breath. "We keep doing what we do. Keep our eyes and ears open. We have extra cameras placed in every nook and cranny we can think of, and the townspeople are also talkin' and more vigilant about outsiders."

Around the table, heads nod.

"Now, let's talk about our other piece of business. This young woman we have in our clubhouse who says she is Blake's sister." Jake swivels in his chair to face me. "I take it you believe her?"

I shrug. "I have no reason not to. My father wasn't faithful. Him knockin' another woman up wouldn't be a shocker."

"I didn't like how she reacted to my presence. The fact that she's conditioned to speak only if spoken to around club members means she's very familiar with the lifestyle. She's young, can't be no more than sixteen, which means she ran off."

"And someone will come looking for her." Tension builds at the base of my skull. I may have gained a sister, but she carries with her things better left in the past. "What if—"

Jake quickly interrupts. "Then we will deal with it. Together. As a club. As your family." He leans forward on his chair. "You got me?"

"I got you." I maintain eye contact with him.

"Good." He jerks his chin. "Go get your sister. We need to have a chat."

I knew this part was coming. I stand then walk out of the room. No one is in the common area, but I hear chattering from the kitchen, so I head in that direction. There, I find all the women and my sister gathered around the table.

"Hey, Blake," Grace greets with a warm smile, and I acknowledge her with a nod.

My eyes fall on my sister. "Bellamy."

She puts her cup on the table. "Yeah?"

"Prez needs to talk with you," I say, and her face falls. "You're not in any trouble, kiddo."

Bella places her hand on Bellamy's forearm. "You've got nothing to be afraid of, sweetie. Jake is a kind man. All of them are good men."

Bellamy pushes up from the table and walks over. Before leaving the kitchen, I seek out Ember, making eye contact. Her smile calms the chaos inside my head. Too soon, I pull my attention from her beautiful face, shift my focus to my sister, and escort her to Church.

I pause outside the door. "You aware of what's about to happen?"

"Yes."

"We need a few answers, kiddo. Just be honest. Nothing you say goes beyond those four walls unless you want it to, all right?"

Bellamy takes a cleansing breath, preparing herself to face my brothers. "Okay."

I open the door and guide her inside. She scans the room, glancing at each set of eyes staring back at her. I pull my chair out for her to sit, then stand behind her, putting my hand on her shoulder for support.

Jake's eyes soften. "How you doin' sweetheart?"

"I'm okay."

"Good. I'm not going to drag this out. What do you say we start with the basics?" Jake asks, and Bellamy nods. "What's your full name and age?" Jake eases back in his seat.

"Bellamy Adeline Steele. I'm fifteen."

Jake's eyes shift from Bellamy to me. I swallow hard. Steele is my dead father's last name. He looks back at my sister. "Where do you live?"

She fidgets with a small mood ring, twisting it on her finger. "Just outside San Bernardino, with my mom and her sleazy boyfriend." She tenses at the mention of her mother's boyfriend, and I don't like it.

"You mentioned not being allowed to speak about club members. Who are you referring to?"

"The club my dad belonged to, Satan's Hounds."

Jake continues his questioning. "What was your dad's name?

"Hudson Steele, but everyone called him Grim," Bellamy says, and I go numb. I haven't heard my father's name in a long time. I don't carry his name; *Birth father* is blank on my birth certificate. I'm thankful to carry my mother's last name Mancini.

Jake keeps his facial expression neutral and crosses his arms over his chest. "You know anything about his death?"

I wasn't expecting him to ask that question. I feel the heavy weight of everyone's stares as he waits for Bellamy's reply. Every man in this room knows the answer to that question.

"Um, just that someone killed him." She shakes her head. "But I have no idea how." Then she mumbles, "Not that I care either way." My sister bows her head, places her hands in her lap, and draws deep breaths. "My father wasn't a good man. None of the Satan's Hounds men are."

I sense her shutting down. By the concerned looks on the other men's faces, so do they. I step to her side and kneel. "Bellamy." I wait for her to look at me. She slowly lifts her face. "Has anyone put their filthy hands on you?" I swear to all that is holy; I will kill any motherfucker who dared. Bellamy's eyes glisten with held-back emotions, yet she manages to keep the tears at bay.

"Not yet."

It takes a hell of a lot of willpower to maintain my composure, because all I want to do right now is put my fist through a wall. I won't lose control of my emotions, though. Not in front of my younger sister. The look in her eyes speaks volumes about the shit she's been through, and from personal experience with Satan's

Hounds, I fucking hate knowing the possibilities. "You're never going back, understand?" I'll be damned. Life may have failed her until now, but she has me now. I won't let anything happen to her.

Bellamy nods. "Yeah," she says softly.

"Not going to sugar coat it, but you're a minor with a mother who is bound to be lookin' for ya, sweetheart. And as bad as we all don't want to see you go back, chances are, it will happen."

I rise. "Over my dead body."

Jake cuts his eyes to me. "Rein it in." His voice is stern, letting me know he's addressing me as Prez, not Jake. "You may be her brother, but that holds no weight in the eyes of the law, should her mother come after her." Jake gives me a second to absorb his words before continuing. He shifts his attention back to my sister. "Sweetheart, I don't like what I said any more than you do, but we have a real problem on our hands should your mother come looking for you. Does she know where you've gone?"

Bellamy moves in her seat. "She probably has no idea I'm even gone." The sadness in her voice further proves that the people in her life who are supposed to care don't.

"How'd you even know where to find Blake?" Logan chimes in, and she looks across the table at him.

"My mom's boyfriend, who is the club's enforcer, tends to have loose lips when he's drinking and talks about club business around my mom. Most of the time, she's too wasted to understand what he's talking about." Bellamy casts her eyes to the table and shrugs. "The walls in our house are thin, so I tend to hear a lot, whether I want to or not." She falls silent.

"Go on." I encourage her to continue.

She sighs. "Boner, that's my mom's boyfriend's name..." My sister pauses when Quinn chuckles, which causes Jake to cut his eyes at my brother with a glare.

Quinn clears his throat. "Sorry."

It's barely audible, but Bellamy giggles at Quinn's amusement. "His real name is Trevor Peterson. Anyway, he, my mom, and a couple of other club members were partying a couple of nights ago, all hitting the whiskey and smoking weed pretty hard for hours. As usual, I stayed locked in my bedroom, avoiding the creepy stares I get from most of the men in the club." Bellamy hugs herself and takes another cleansing breath. "Boner started rambling on about the good old days when my dad was alive, which eventually led to him going on about..." Her voice wavers, apprehensive about continuing. She looks back at me. "I'm sorry," she whispers, then faces Jake. "He started talking about how my dad was a stone-cold badass. That my dad was the only man he knew who could kill his kid's mother for stealing five hundred bucks and leaving his ass in the dead of night." Bellamy sniffles then her emotions get the better of her, and tears stream down her face.

Heat spreads through my chest, and I fist my hands at my sides. Pent-up rage and grief are brewing as I think about the day my father took my life away. I find myself battling the overwhelming need to hurt someone, destroy something, or run. Bellamy shoots out of her chair and wraps her arms around my waist.

"I'm sorry he took so much from you." She's straight-up crying now.

I pull myself together, because none of this is about just me anymore. It's about us. "He paid the price for his sins." I pull back and look down at her tear-stained face. "Don't ever apologize for that motherfucker. And please don't cry for me, Bellamy. I've lost a lot in my life, but I've gained a hell of a lot too. You standing in front of me right now proves that, despite the hell we go through, good things happen too."

Bellamy smiles at me. "Are you always this optimistic?"

"No," the men answer in unison with me. It's true that I'm more of a glass-half-empty man. The men fall silent, waiting. "You okay to continue?" I ask her.

"Yeah." She dries her face with the backs of her hands, then turns around and returns her attention to my brothers. "The other members there that night told him to shut the fuck up, which he did, but only for a little while. Boner started talking again. He went on about how Hellhound, the club's president, told him he found out Grim's son was living in Polson, Montana, and was associated with the local MC, and that he'd been keeping tabs on him."

We look at each other and our faces harden with the news that another MC has been watching us, me specifically. *What the fuck would my uncle want with me?* Only one reason comes to mind.

Bellamy sinks into the seat again and shakes her head. "At first, I couldn't believe what I'd heard. I mean, how could I trust a strung-out drunk's words? But something deep inside of me told me I needed to find out. It wasn't long after overhearing all this I noticed the house grow quiet. I ventured out of my room because I was hungry. Everyone was passed out except for my mom, who was stumbling back into the living room." She shrugs. "When I looked at her, all I could think of was I have a brother and wanted to know if she knew anything. I grabbed her by the arm, made her look at me, and asked her point-blank if she knew I had a brother. Her speech was slurred, but she managed to admit that she knew. Then I asked if she knew my brother's name, and she said it was Blaze, Blake, or something like that. Once my mom passed out with the rest of them, I threw whatever I could into a backpack. I took some cash out of Boner's wallet, walked down to the corner, called an Uber to the bus station, then bought myself a one-way ticket."

"You've got balls stealing from an MC member," Gabriel observes.

"I was less afraid of stealing from Boner and taking my chances on the unknown than sticking around there any longer," Bellamy admits, holding her own against Gabriel's heavy stare.

"How did you find Blake? More specifically, how did you find the compound?"

My sister looks down the table at Reid and says matter-of-factly, "The internet. All I had to do was type in Motorcycle Club Polson Montana, and bam, there you are, Kings of Retribution MC. You have a Louisiana chapter too. You guys do many charity drives, also. Once I got to town, I got an Uber driver. He freaked when he asked where I was going, but an extra hundred bucks persuaded him not to cancel the ride."

"You got grit." Jake nods, impressed by her fearlessness and determination. "I think that's enough for today. I appreciate you being so forthcoming, Bellamy." Jake scrubs his beard. "I'll also need you to hand over your phone."

Bellamy doesn't question why. She reaches into her pocket and places her phone on the table. "You can return to whatever you were doing before," Jake adds.

"Can I still stay?" She eyes Jake.

"You can stay," Jake assures her.

Once my sister is out of the room, I face my brothers. Out of all the information she disclosed, I'm still stuck on knowing that my father's brother knows my whereabouts. "What's our next move?" Logan leans forward, resting his forearms against the surface of the table.

"We hit this head-on. We need to know their motive for hunting down Blake's location and just how long they've known. This means we make the first move and let them know they're on our radar too."

"What if they're lookin' for trouble—for retaliation?" My thoughts shift to Ember. Just as I've decided to stop living in the cold shadow of my father to have a future with the woman I love, my past finds a way to fucking ruin it all.

"Then we deal with it," Jake asserts.

"Even if that means war? I won't put the club in danger because the devil is out to collect his dues because I killed my father."

Jake stands and slams his fist against the table. "If Satan's Hounds come lookin' for a fight, we'll give them one." He points his finger around the table. "Look at them." My brothers stand, and our President continues, "We are your family. Just as you will die for one of us, we will die for you."

12

EMBER

"How did you and Jake meet?"

Blake and I have been lying in bed in comfortable silence, neither of us hurrying to start the day.

I roll over and face him.

"What made you come to Polson and join the club?" I counter.

I study him for a beat, but his face has no judgmental look and no underlying tone in his question—only curiosity.

"I met Jake at a bar not far outside of Nevada. He was there with Doc."

Blake looks thoughtful for a minute. "I remember when you first arrived. That was around when Prez and Doc went to see an old buddy in Vegas. But you came to live at the club a month or so after."

I nod. "Yeah, I lived with Lisa and Doc for a while before I decided to live at the clubhouse." I sigh. "It's not like I woke up one morning and decided to be a whore, right?"

Blake's face goes hard, and I immediately regret my snippy attitude.

"You know I don't think of you that way, so I never want to hear you fuckin' talk like that about yourself again," he fumes.

"I'm sorry." I bring my hand up to his chest. "I'm just so used to getting defensive when people question why I live the way I do. I know you're not judging me, and I shouldn't have made it seem like you do."

"I'm the last person to judge how another person chooses to live their life, Emb—"

At the word *choose*, I cut Blake off by yelling, "My boyfriend lost a card game, and when he couldn't pay, he offered me up instead!"

Blake's body tenses. "The fuck?" he growls.

"We grew up together. Our parents were friends, and we ran in the same social circle. My parents approved of him because of his family's social status." I roll my eyes at how cliché this all sounds. "They didn't know I was only with him because he hooked me up with booze and got me into the best parties and clubs. I mean; everyone knew about his gambling problem. His parents had to bail him out more than once when he got in way over his head with the wrong people. But, he had the right last name and came from money, so my parents looked the other way."

I close my eyes and think back to that night at the bar. My body shudders when I remember how the guy smiled at me when Devan chose his car over me. "Anyway, Devan decided he wanted to go to Vegas on a whim. I, being stupid, said I would go with. A few days into our trip, we stopped at some seedy-looking dive. All was good at first. Sure, some sketchy-looking dudes were there, but they didn't bother us, and we didn't bother them. That all changed when Devan decided to invite himself into their card game. My boyfriend didn't have the money to pay those men, which made the situation turn ugly. One of the men mentioned they'd noticed what kind of car we arrived in and agreed to take that instead. Devan threw a fit over his precious car, so the guy said for Devan to choose between his car or his girlfriend."

I pause and look at Blake, who hasn't spoken during my retelling. He looks like he's about to blow a fuse, but I continue. "The asshole chose his car." I shake my head. "To this day, I still can't believe anyone would choose a stupid car over a human being." Now I'm getting worked up all over again. "I knew Devan didn't love me, just like I didn't love him, but I would have never done something like that. Surely, he had to have known those guys' intentions with me. The jerk was more worried about what his daddy would do if he lost his car." I pause when I feel the fury rolling off Blake in waves and decide to move on to the part of my story that ends with me rescued by Jake. Just thinking about it makes me smile. "You should have seen those assholes' faces when Jake showed up out of nowhere with his gun drawn."

Blake visibly relaxes at the mention of Jake and a small smile tugs at his lips.

"He told those guys he was walking out of that bar with me, and he'd kill anyone who tried to stop him." I let out a small laugh.

"What made you go with Prez? What made you feel you could trust him?" Blake asks.

"His eyes," I tell him. "At first glance, Jake was this huge, burly biker with a presence that screamed danger. But one look in his eyes and I knew I could trust him. I felt safe. Safer than I had ever felt in my life. Something about Jake made me feel like everything would be okay." I bite my bottom lip. "Sounds stupid, doesn't it? There I was about to be taken against my will by sleazy bikers, but without hesitation, I left with another, not knowing who he was or his true intentions."

Blake wraps his arm around me and pulls me closer to his chest. "It doesn't sound stupid at all, baby. You listened to your gut. And in your case, it worked out."

"Yeah," I whisper, laying my head on his chest. After a moment of silence, I continue. "After hauling ass away from the bar, Jake rode around for about thirty minutes, taking back roads until he stopped at a gas station. He asked me where home was and a little about myself. He offered to give me some cash and put me on a plane home, or I could ride back to Montana with him. It wasn't a hard choice to make."

I prop my chin on the back of my hand and look at Blake. "When we got to Polson, he took me straight to Lisa's. Doc must have already told her what had happened, because she was expecting me. For a month, I battled with myself over what to do. I knew I didn't want to go home, but I also felt guilt over leaving my sister and parents. It didn't go well when I finally got the guts to call my mom and dad. It turned out Devan had gotten to them before me and fed them a completely different story than what had happened. According to his rendition, I dumped him and left of my own free will with those bikers. He basically painted me as a slut and him as the victim."

"You fuckin' serious?" Blake's nostrils flare.

"Oh yeah. The last words I spoke with my father were him calling me a disgraceful slut."

"Babe, that's fucked up. I have in mind to haul my ass to Georgia."

"It's not even worth it, honey."

"The fuck it's not."

"Blake, you think I care what they or anyone else thinks of me?" I shake my head. "I'm not saying I'm immune to the hurtfulness of it all, but I have learned that someone else's negative opinion of me is not my problem." I grin. "I do see the irony in my situation. My father called me a slut when, in fact, I was the furthest thing from it. Then I went on to become a club girl." Blake grinds his molars, but I continue before he can get onto me again. "I'm not ashamed of my role in this club, Blake, and I'm not putting myself down. I love my life. I love everything about the club. You, Jake, the guys, and the girls all get me. Being here has given me a chance to find myself. There was never any pressure to be or do anything other than what made me happy. There are no expectations to live up to. Now, look at me. It's taken a few years, but I finally found my passion, which doesn't require two college degrees."

Blake drags his hand through my hair and grips my neck. "I'm so fuckin' proud of you, baby."

His praise brings a massive smile to my face. "I'm proud of myself too."

Blake grins. "It's about damn time everyone else found out."

"What do you mean everyone else?"

Blake lifts a brow.

"Wait!" I sit up. "Did you know?"

He chuckles. "Baby, I've known for a while."

"How long?"

He shrugs. "A year or so. I found out when the second book in the Montana Lights series was released."

"Oh my god! Why didn't you say anything?"

"Because you held that part of your life close to your heart for whatever reason. I knew you'd share when you were ready."

"Thank you." I lean forward and touch my lips to his. Gripping my ass, Blake maneuvers me to straddle his hips. I moan into his mouth when my center touches his hard cock beneath the sheets. "We're going to miss breakfast," I say around his lips.

"I'm pretty fuckin' hungry." Blake reaches for the hem of my t-shirt and pulls it off over my head. "But not for food."

"Oh yeah?" I breathe. "What did you have in mind?"

Blake gets a wicked gleam in his eyes as he shoves his palms underneath my butt and begins pulling me up his body. "Your sweet pussy. Now be a good girl and sit on my face."

When Blake and I finally leave the bedroom, the clubhouse is full of activity. I can hear Bella's laughter along with Logan's voice. As I cross the threshold into the main room and see everyone there, I turn on my heel, running smack into Blake's chest. "Is it too late to run and hide?" I mumble into his shirt. His body shakes with silent laughter.

"Heifer!"

"Fuck," I curse at the sound of Glory's voice. Turning around, I try and fail to hold back a smile when I meet her gaze. "Good morning to you, too, Glory."

"Morning?" She looks down at her watch. "Try afternoon. My ass has been waiting for you two to come up for air for the past two hours."

"We tried to hold them back as long as possible, darlin'," Quinn calls out from the corner of the room.

"What are you even talking about?" Emerson stands with her hand on her hip. "I'm not the one who has had my nose buried in that book for two days."

Embarrassment washes over me, and I notice something in Quinn's hand. "What is that?" I point.

Quinn freezes. "What's what?"

"That book you're reading?"

Quinn suddenly looks like he's a kid that's been caught with his hand in the cookie jar. "You see, what had happened was..."

He doesn't get the chance to finish his explanation when I charge him. Running across the room, I hop on the coffee table and leap onto Quinn's back. "Give me that!"

"No! It's mine!" He holds it up out of my reach.

"Hot damn! Now, this was worth getting up early for!" Glory cheers. "Get him, girl."

"Jesus Christ." Emerson shakes her head. "I swear I can't take his ass anywhere."

"Hey, you're supposed to be on my side, Sunshine."

Emerson rolls her eyes. "I don't know you."

Taking advantage of his distraction, I jab Quinn in the ribs and snatch the book from his hands. When I get back to my feet, I turn and give him the stink eye.

"That wasn't cool," he grumbles, rubbing at where I poked him.

From the other side of the room, I hear Gabriel rumble, "Estúpido."

"Quinn, what is this?" I flip through the pages and see several paragraphs highlighted in yellow. "Did you highlight all the sex scenes?"

"Seriously." Emerson holds up her hand. "I don't know him."

"You knew me last night when I acted out page seventy-six on you," Quinn says.

"Oh my god!" Emerson and I cry at the same time. If I looked in a mirror right now, I'm positive my face would be as red as Quinn's wife's.

"This is getting good. I need wine." Glory rubs her hands together with giddiness.

"Glory," Bella jests. "It's not even noon."

Glory counters, "Mimosas then?"

"I don't know why you're acting all embarrassed," Quinn quips. "This book is the shit. Besides, thousands of people read your books every day."

"Yeah, but I don't know those people. Knowing you've read this; how am I supposed to look you, of all people, in the eye?" I hold the book up. "And that you two—" I gesture between Quinn and Emerson "—have been," I say slowly, scrunching up my nose, "inspired."

Emerson raises her hand. "I vote we forget all about this and never speak on it again."

We all look at Bella, who is typing away on her phone. Sensing our eyes on her, she looks up. "What?"

Emerson glares at her.

"I only told Mila, Grace, and Sofia," she confesses.

Emerson crosses her arms over her chest.

Bella hangs her head and mumbles, "And Easton."

"What!" Emerson shouts. "This is not the kind of ammunition my brother needs. He will never let me live this down."

Alba, who has been silent through the fiasco, cackles.

Quinn strides up to me. "Look, all jokes aside, your books are great." He pulls me into his side and kisses the top of my head. "And I, for one, am fuckin' proud of you, darlin'."

I slump against him and smile. "Thanks, Quinn. That means a lot."

After a moment, he asks, "Can I have my book back? On page one-twenty-three, Jackson does this thing to Aubrey that—"

I cut him off by slapping the book against his stomach. "Please stop."

Quinn gives me a boyish grin before striding toward Emerson still pouting at the bar.

"Hey," Glory protests. "I wanted to know what was on page one-twenty-three."

"Forget page one-twenty-three." Alba reaches into her bag and pulls out the same paperback Quinn has. "Seventy-six will give you butterflies. And I'm not talking about the kind you get in your tummy."

"Alba!" Bella gasps at her sister in shock. "I don't want to hear my little sister talk like that."

Alba rolls her eyes. "You do know I'm grown."

"I know. But you're still my little sister, and my ears don't want to be assaulted by your dirty talk."

Alba huffs, "You're one to talk. I hear the x-rated things Logan whispers in your ear. And you say I'm dirty?"

"I think everyone needs to stop talking." I rub my temples. "This is just too weird."

"Wait!" Alba gasps, ignoring my idea to stop talking. "Ember." She rushes up to me. "You must come to the bookstore and sign at our grand opening."

I freeze. "What?"

"It will be perfect," she continues. "We'll set up a table, and you can sign customer copies."

"Alba, I'm not sure I'm ready for that."

"Please, Ember," she begs. "At least agree to think about it."

"Fine," I sigh. "I'll think about it."

Alba's face lights with excitement. I'm not winning this battle, because she will relentlessly bug me until she gets what she wants.

From behind, Blake drapes his arm across my chest. "Do you want to go for a ride with me?"

My body relaxes against his, and I nod. "What about your sister?"

"Reid, Logan, Mila, and Bella are taking their kids and Remi to the lake today. Remi invited Bellamy. That's all she could talk about last night."

I smile. "Remi has taken Bellamy under her wing, and I like that for her."

"Me too. I don't think she had many friends before."

I quickly steer his focus toward something else when I notice Blake's mood slipping in a different direction at the mention of his sister's life before finding us.

"Since we have all afternoon, will you take me up the mountain?"

Blake kisses the sensitive spot below my ear, his stubble making my skin prickle. "Yeah, Vita Mia, I'll take you up the mountain."

13

BLAKE

It's early morning, and we're all sitting around the table, guzzling coffee and chowing down on some of Grace's freshly baked lemon-blueberry muffins with the cheesecake filling. "Hey, kiddo. What do you say you, Ember, and I spend the day together?"

"Really?" My sister's face lights up. Since her arrival, we haven't gotten the chance to get to know one another, aside from what we revealed during her questions with Jake the other day.

"Yeah. Ember can pack us lunch and drive out to my place." I hurry up and snatch the last one from the box before Quinn wraps his gluttonous fingers around it.

"Come on, man. Those are my favorite," Quinn pouts.

"Everything you eat is your favorite." Ember laughs.

"I'm beginning to think his insatiable hunger is due to an oral fixation." Emerson sets a plate of crispy bacon in front of her man. "This should keep your mouth busy."

Quinn wraps his arm around her hip, grabbing a handful of her ass and tugging her close. "I don't hear you complaining when you're the one benefiting from my gluttonous tendencies." He waggles his brows, and Emerson rolls her eyes, though a smile tugs at her lips.

"Your powers are greatly exaggerated." Emerson smirks at Quinn, clearly fucking with him, but knowing my brother, he'll take her jesting as a challenge.

He stands, hand resting on Emerson's hip, and his face takes on a more serious expression. "We'll see about that." He bends at the knees and hoists her over his shoulder, causing Emerson to laugh loudly.

"Quinn!" she squeals, smacking her palm against his ass. "Put me down!"

"Shut it. I'm about to remind you of my superpowers, babe." Quinn begins to walk away from the table but stops himself long enough to snatch up the plate of bacon, then strolls out of the kitchen, passing Nikolai, who is walking into the room. "Hey, brother," Quinn greets Nikolai as he brushes by him.

Nikolai watches the pair disappear, then walks further into the kitchen. "What's that all about?" Nikolai chuckles.

"Sex, bacon, and superpowers." I shake my head.

"You have the best family," Bellamy chimes in.

"They're your family, too, kiddo." I nudge her with my shoulder. I look over at Nikolai. "Hey, brother. I heard you and Reid landed the hospital job."

"Yeah. We break ground in two weeks." He pours himself a mug of coffee. "Logan around?"

"Jake sent him and Gabriel out to make rounds around town." I down the rest of my coffee, push my chair from the table, and take my dirty dishes to the sink. For the past couple of days, we've all been keeping a closer eye on things, which involves riding the streets of Polson from one end of town to the other in pairs, each of us taking shifts throughout the day while we wait to hear that we've made contact with Satan's Hounds.

"Who's that?" Bellamy whispers to Ember. "He's hot."

"That's Nikolai," Ember murmurs.

"He is way too old for you and married," I say without giving much thought, and Bellamy blushes, immediately tearing her gaze away from Nikolai in embarrassment.

"Blake," Ember chastises me.

Nikolai approaches the table. "You must be the sister I've heard about." He smiles down at Bellamy. "I'm Nikolai, Logan's brother."

"Oh. You're a club member too?" Bellamy takes him in, clearly noticing he isn't wearing a leather cut.

"No. Just my brother, Logan."

"Oh." She nods. "My name is Bellamy." She flashes a friendly smile at Nikolai. "You have an accent. Are you Russian?"

"Yes." Nikolai grins.

"OHchen' priYATna."

Nikolai, Ember, and I look at Bellamy, who just spoke what sounded like Russian. Nikolai smiles in amazement. "OHchen' priYATna. Impressive. You know Russian?"

She shrugs as if it's nothing. "A little. Other languages and cultures are beautiful and fascinating to me. I spent a lot of time alone in my room back home, so, with nothing better to do, I watched and listened to videos online. I've taught myself some Russian, Spanish, and Chinese, but only basic greetings and how to ask where the bathroom is located."

"What did you say to Nikolai?" My curiosity gets the better of me.

"Roughly translated, it means nice to meet you," Nikolai answers before my sister.

"Bellamy, that's amazing," Ember praises my sister.

"It's nothing special." Bellamy's hair shrouds her face when she looks down at her plate and pushes pieces of scrambled egg around with a fork.

"Yes, it is," Ember, Nikolai, and I say at the same time.

Nikolai sighs, placing his mug on the counter. "I've got to run. Tell Logan I'll catch up with him another time." Nikolai then gives his attention to my sister, "Welcome to the family, Bellamy." Then he takes his leave.

My sister breathes when Nikolai is no longer in the kitchen. "The men around here are fine."

"I can't hear you say things like that."

She laughs. "Why?"

"Because." I stand and try coming up with a good reason other than she's my sister. Because how can I play the big brother card after only a few days of knowing she exists? "You're fifteen."

Bellamy rolls her eyes. "I have eyes, Blake."

I glance at Ember, who appears amused at my clumsy brotherly behavior. "For it to only be your third day of playing the part of big brother, I would say you are falling into the role naturally." She bites her lip to suppress a smile.

"I'm duckin' out of this conversation before I get myself in trouble." I stride over to Ember, lean down, and cover her mouth with mine. "I'll be outside."

She smiles against my lips as I give her another kiss. "Okay. Bellamy and I will hang out, and we'll go ahead and prepare some sandwiches and pack up some of Bella's leftover potato salad for lunch. Come get us when you're ready to leave."

With one final taste of her lips, I stroll out of the kitchen and head outside to where my beat-up old pickup truck is parked. I open the passenger side door and grab the toolbox from the floorboard. Moving to the front, I lift the rusty hood of my 1965 Dodge. I bought the truck from Charley last spring. It had been sitting in his garage for several years, and he had no time to fix her. He loved the truck and hated to see it go, but selling it to me gave him peace of mind. She doesn't look like much now, but once I finally get her into the shop and repaint the body to its original pine-green color, everything about her will be restored. I lean under the hood and begin replacing the spark plugs.

Once finished, I wipe the grime from my hands onto a shop rag as I walk around to the driver's side, then slide in and turn the engine over. On the second try, she fires right up. I let the motor run while I put my tools away and close the hood. The rumble of bikes draws my attention, and I look toward the compound gate and see Logan and Gabriel are back. I toss the toolbox into the truck's bed, turn the motor off, and head inside to wash up before we gather for church.

Church commences once we've all taken a seat. "How were the roads this mornin'?" Jake directs his attention to Logan and Gabriel.

"Nothin' to report," Logan states, and beside him, Gabriel sits silently with his arms folded over his chest.

Jake nods. "Let's hope it remains that way." His jaw tightens, and the energy in the room changes. "Contact has been made with Satan's Hounds, and they've agreed to a sit-down. The face-to-face will occur in a small town straddling the Utah-Nevada state line."

Austin leans forward. "That's at least a full day's ride, depending on the weather."

"It is, but this needs to take place on neutral territory. I won't have a fuckin' Satan's Hound stepping foot in my town." Jake's voice hardens. "These fuckers are known to be unpredictable and backstabbing. This club doesn't live by any code, and rules of conduct don't mean jack shit to them."

"We know their numbers?" Quinn asks, and Reid chimes in to answer his question.

"Around a dozen." Reid sighs, adding, "These guys are into shady shit. Aside from manufacturing and selling street drugs and theft, they've had their hands in human trafficking and are rumored to be associated with cartels."

I take in all the information Reid supplies, and guilt continues eating at my insides. Karma is a sick motherfucker, and he's looking to collect on my sins.

"Blake," Jake barks, jolting me from my intrusive thinking, and I cut my eyes to him and can tell he knows where my head is. "I need you in the right headspace goin' into this. You got me?"

"Yeah."

"Good, because you'll be joinin' me, Logan, Gabriel, and Quinn for this sit down." Jake looks down at the table at Reid. "Reid, I'll need you, Austin, and Grey to hold the place down. If you need anything, contact Demetri. He agreed to assist in any way should the club run into trouble while the rest of us are away."

"Should we be on lockdown for the time being?" Grey asks.

Jake ponders Grey's question, scrubbing his beard, then shakes his head. "Not until we leave. But while we're out of pocket, I want the women and children to camp out here until our return. They are free to leave the compound if they report where they're going and check in once they reach their destination. Our women are already aware there's shit that we're handling, and they're being cautious of their surroundings."

"When do we leave?" Gabriel finally speaks.

"We ride out in a few days," Jake states.

Just before noon, I load the cooler of food Ember and Bellamy packed for our lunch today into the back of the pickup, along with a large quilt and a new chainsaw I bought several days ago. Hearing footsteps, I look over my shoulder to see my sister approaching.

"What's the chainsaw for?"

"We're heading to my property up the mountain. I work up there when I have time."

"Cutting down trees?" Bellamy tilts her head.

I chuckle. "Somethin' like that. I carve art pieces out of trees."

Her eyes widen. "Chainsaw carving?"

"Yeah." I close the tailgate.

"That's so cool." She opens the passenger side door and climbs into the truck's cab.

The clubhouse door swings open. "I'm ready, finally." Ember steps outside. "Couldn't decide on what to wear. Does this look okay?" she asks. I drink her in as she walks toward me wearing a short black cherry print summer dress. The sweetheart neckline enhances the fullness of her breasts. She's got her hair down in loose curls. My eyes travel down her bare legs, the short hem showing her colorful thigh tattoos. I smile at the sneakers on her feet and snake my arm around her waist when she's within reach. "Come here."

"Too much for a picnic?" she asks.

"You're perfect, Vita Mia," I assure her.

"You sure we should be leaving?"

"I already cleared it with Prez, baby," I assure her. "Now get that sweet ass in the truck."

Hours later, we're relaxing in the sun as we sit on the blanket on the ground. I take a deep breath of the fresh pine mountain air, more content than I've felt in a long time. Over the day spent up here, I've gotten to know my sister better. She loves reading, which inspired an hour-long discussion between her and Ember. She loves black and hates pink. She's obsessed with the TV series Supernatural, which I can get behind. Her ideal man is Jensen Ackles, who plays Dean Winchester. And I now know how to ask where the bathroom is in Chinese. I have yet to share much in return. Very little to tell.

"It's so pretty out here." Bellamy takes a container of cookies from the cooler. "Can I ask you something?" She avoids looking at me.

"Ask away."

"What happened? I mean, with our dad."

I tense. "What do you mean?" I question, needing her to be more specific.

"Why did he do what he did to your mom?"

My mouth becomes dry as the Sahara Desert while my attention shifts to Ember, who eyes me with concern. She doesn't even know the details. She only knows they were murdered. My woman reaches out and lays her hand on my thigh, anchoring me and giving me the strength to tell my story. "You sure you want to know?"

Bellamy nods, crisscrossing her legs, and straightens her back. "I can handle it."

I eye her for a moment and consider that she's only fifteen, even though her eyes hint at her soul being older from growing up too fast. I take a cleansing breath. "Our father wasn't around much during my childhood, and I saw the door slamming on his way out more than I saw him coming in it. Whenever he was around, I was invisible to him. I still don't understand how my mom stayed with him for so long."

"Maybe she felt if she loved him enough, she could fix him, make him a better man," Ember suggests.

I look at Ember. "Some people can't be fixed, baby." My words cause her expression to change. I can't handle the sadness in her eyes and look away, focusing on the lake in the distance. "I would watch him build my mom up just to cut her down. She would beg him to get clean, to stay sober long enough to see the world differently, but he didn't want any part of the pretty little picture she was painting him." I lick my dry lips and feel myself being taken back in time. Pushing through the discomfort, I continue. The only way to get to the other side of the pain is to go through it. "I came home from school one day to find my mom in tears. I was nine then but knew what had happened that day." My stomach tightens, and bile burns my throat from the emotion of that day rising to the surface. "My father allowed his MC brother to have his way with my mom." My nostrils flare as my breathing increases.

"Blake." Ember's hand grips my thigh tighter.

I glance at my sister, whose attention is still on my face. Unshed tears pool in her eyes, but she says nothing.

"I grabbed a gun from my mom's nightstand." I picture the events in my head as I tell what happened. "I wanted to kill him. I had every intention of putting a bullet in him, but I didn't know the gun wasn't loaded, so nothing happened when I pulled the trigger. If it weren't for my mom, I'm positive he would have killed me for what I attempted." I huff and shake my head because I still feel the sting of his words. "The last words we exchanged was him telling me I was nothin' more than a waste of cum..." I fall silent.

"What did you say to him?" Bellamy's voice breaks with emotion.

I lock eyes with my sister. "I promised that one day, I would kill him." Bellamy remains composed. I pause, needing a moment before continuing. "We left that night. She waited until our dad passed out, took several bills from the pile of cash he had on the coffee table, and we walked what felt like miles to the bus station. My mom bought a one-way ticket to a small town outside San Bernardino where the grandparents I'd never met lived. Three months later, our father found us. The aftermath left my mom and grandparents dead. I went into the system soon after. For years my mom's and grandparents' deaths were written off as a robbery gone wrong. They never found evidence leading back to our father, so the case went cold. It wasn't until a few years ago that I learned his club paid off a handful of dirty cops to cover up the murders."

Finally, the tears she had held back slowly fall down her cheeks. "I don't mean to be a baby." She wipes them away.

I hang my head, unsure if I should have shared so much. I feel Ember's hand cup my cheek and guide my face to look at her. Her eyes are also wet with tears, and I feel an ache. "I shouldn't have said anything."

"The bravest thing anyone can do is share their most vulnerable pieces with others. Don't apologize for that, Blake." Her lips press lightly against mine. The kiss is soft but has the strength to lift me.

"I don't think my mom loved our dad," Bellamy says, breaking the connection between Ember and me, though not intentionally. "My mom wasn't always an addict." She takes a deep breath and focuses on the cookie in her hands. I shift my body and pull Ember into my side, where she lays her head on my shoulder, and we give Bellamy our undivided attention. "She used to bake cupcakes all the time and let me help." A small but sad smile tugs at her lips as she remembers the good in her life, but it fades quickly. "I was six years old when she started changing. I would find her passed out on the couch or in her bed. On my 8th birthday, I found her slumped on the bathroom floor with a needle in her arm. Her breathing was shallow. I called 911." She sighs, taking a moment to gather herself. "I went into state custody that summer while my mom left to get better. She had just gotten me back when our dad was killed."

A better person would feel something right about now, knowing they are responsible for a man's death, but I'm not that person.

Bellamy gets to her feet, only to turn her back to us and lift her face to the sun. "For almost a year, she managed to stay clean, but she failed to avoid the club lifestyle and became involved with another club member. She relapsed not long after." She sniffles and faces us. The amount of brokenness I see in her eyes mirrors mine. "I understand your mom having hope, Blake. That somehow, someway, through all odds, you can fix someone. I was convinced I would fix her if I loved her hard enough. And that she would eventually love me enough to stop and take care of me instead, but it never happened." Bellamy claws at her chest. It's clear to me that my sister has been grieving the loss of the mother she once knew for a long time.

I'm on my feet and wrapping my arms around her as she buries her face against my chest and cries, releasing years of tears. Bellamy hiccups. "Why am I not enough?"

"It's not your fault. Addiction doesn't just take from the user. It robs from the people around them, too." I think about my sobriety. "You are enough, Bellamy."

Several minutes pass before she pulls away and takes a few deep breaths.

Ember stands, bringing a bottle of cold water with her, and offers it to Bellamy.

"I feel ridiculous for falling apart," my sister apologizes.

"Don't sweat it, kiddo. I know what it's like to have the world's weight on your shoulders and hurt and anger eating at your insides. It's bound to spill out sometimes." I sigh, feeling some of the weight lifted.

Ember comforts Bellamy, brushing the teen's hair away from her face, "We're allowed to fall apart from time to time." She turns her face toward me, letting me know her words are meant for me, too, then she goes back to focusing on Bellamy.

I stand back and watch the woman I love being so tender to my sister, and suddenly can't help thinking that she'll be the best mom to our kids one day. I latch onto that image momentarily, letting it encapsulate me. Ember has a swollen belly, sitting on the porch swing of the home I built for us on this very spot. We're watching the sunset. She turns her head, looks at me, and smiles, rubbing circles on her pregnant belly and saying, "I love you."

She's my person—the one I want to spend the rest of my life with. There are no doubts that I'm in love with her.

"Hey." Ember's touch causes the vision to fade, and she stands before me. "Where did you go?"

"Nowhere." My heart is racing as I continue thinking about the future.

She eyes me with concern. "You, okay?"

"I'm good."

She studies me for a beat longer, then smiles. "Then what do you say to the three of us catching the beginning of a beautiful sunset before heading back?"

I dip my head, hovering my mouth over hers. "I'm a lucky man," I declare. Before my lips touch hers, I add, "You're mine."

Ember smiles. "Damn right I am."

When we get back, night has fallen, and activities around the clubhouse are minimal. Except for the older kids hanging out downstairs, everyone else is settled in for the night, and the place is quiet. I peel my shirt over my head, toss it to the floor, and kick off my boots. I sit in the chair beside the window and recline, watching Ember slip out of her clothes. My gaze fixates on her as she moves about the room, taking in the flare of her hips and the way her tits sway with each step she takes. She's confident in her skin, and that makes her more attractive. My dick stiffens as she lights the candles in the bedroom one at a time before turning out the light. The flames flicker, casting shadows on the walls and a warm glow on the ceiling. My eyes land on her cello. "Play for me." My voice is deep, needing to touch her.

Ember smiles, and without hesitating, she retrieves her instrument. "Sit," I spread my legs, and she steps between them and sits. Parting her knees, she places the cello between her thighs and positions her fingers. Before she drags her bow across the strings, I lean in, pressing my chest against her back. "No matter what, don't stop until the song is over." I kiss her neck, causing her to gasp. "Play for me, Vita Mia."

Ember begins to play, her fingers traveling along the metal

strings as she strokes the bow across them, creating the haunting, sensual melody "Wicked Games." The tune itself is hypnotizing. I pepper kisses across her shoulder while tracing my fingers down her ribcage, softly caressing the sides of her breasts. I palm both tits, thumbing over her nipples, feeling them harden. Ember continues to play, not wavering. I kiss and nip at her neck as my touch travels farther down her body. My hand dips between her thighs, finding her slick with arousal. I play her like she plays the cello. Ember's head falls back against my chest, her breathing increasing with each stroke against her clit. Her thighs clench against the sides of her instrument, and she moans. "That's it." Her body quivers, letting me know she's close. Her bow drags across the strings one last time while she simultaneously cries out my name as her body quakes with orgasms.

While she's riding the high, I grab her cello and set it to the side. I unzip my fly and take out my cock. "Ride me." My voice is husky. Ember stands and turns to face me. I stroke my dick as she straddles me. The tip of my cock grazes her entrance just before she sinks. I hiss as she begins to move, rotating her hips. I spread my legs wider, making hers do the same, opening her more.

"Oh, god," Ember moans, and I do it again.

I dip my head and suck a nipple into my mouth. Ember's fingers tangle in my hair, fisting it in her hands when I switch to the other breast and give it equal attention.

I snake an arm around her waist, bringing our bodies closer together. Our breathing is heavy as our lips are pressed together. I can feel the thud of our combined heartbeats as we share one breath. The world around us doesn't exist. It's just her and me. The moment her sweet pussy tightens, strangling the fuck out of my dick as an orgasm ravages her body, I lose it and explode.

Ember's movements are slow. For a moment, our heavy breathing is the only sound heard. Our bodies, wet with sweat, are cooled by the breeze drifting through the cracked window. I lock eyes with her, gripping her neck and placing her palm against my chest, right over my still-pounding heart. "Some people search their whole lives to find what I've found." A beat of silence hangs between us. "I love you, Vita Mia," I confess.

"I love you too, Blake."

14

EMBER

With the increased activity here at the clubhouse, I've had little opportunity for personal time. Blake is taking the day to spend some one-on-one time with Bellamy, so I'm finally able to catch up on some much-needed writing and responding to a backlog of emails. I finish putting in a large order for paperbacks. Though I have yet to say yes to Alba, I've decided to have my first signing at Leah's and her store. It's time to take that leap. I'm nervous just thinking about putting myself out there but excited at the same time. Even though it's been over a year since I started this journey, I wake up each morning feeling like it's all a dream. Knowing the people I care for the most are proud of me and support me one hundred percent means the world and helps keep me moving forward.

When I first came to the club, I felt lost. I needed direction. I stumbled through life, searching for what I wanted. The only thing I knew for sure was I didn't like the life my mom and dad had been pressuring me to lead.

Here, there is never any pressure, time limit, or expectations When Jake found out about my writing, he looked at me like I'd dreamed my father would look at me. The five words he told me, *I never had a doubt*, still choke me up.

A knock on my bedroom door brings me out of my thoughts. I turn to see Blake standing there with Bellamy. "Hey, baby."

I smile. "Hey. I thought you two already left."

"We're headed out now." He walks farther into the room and stops at my desk. "Are you sure you don't want to come along?"

"Yeah, Ember. It's going to be fun. Blake is taking me to see the new Marvel movie and then to get ice cream," Bellamy says with sheer excitement.

"I have tons of work to catch up on. But you two have fun and bring me back some cookie dough, would ya?"

"Okay," she chirps, then takes off down the hall, making Blake chuckle.

"We'll be back in a bit, babe." He leans down and plants a kiss on my lips.

Once Blake leaves, I turn back to my computer and open the email from my editor. I scan the notes she left on my manuscript. There's another knock at my door, followed by Bellamy calling for me. "Um, Ember. Blake says there's someone here to see you."

Scrunching my brow, I wrack my brain to think who could be here to see me. Pushing off the desk, I pad down the hall until I hear a familiar voice. "No freaking way!" I pick up the pace. When I clear the hall, I first see Blake's large frame. The second he sees me, Blake steps aside, revealing someone I haven't seen in years.

"Em!" my little sister screeches. Dropping her bag, she runs at me.

"Scarlett!" As soon as my sister is within reach, we wrap our arms around each other in the most brutal embrace. "Oh, my God! What—" I cut myself off and look at my baby sister from head to toe. "What are you doing here?"

"I did it." She starts to cry.

"Did what?" I ask, wiping away the tears from her cheeks.

"I left."

"Left?"

Scarlett nods. "Yesterday morning, I told Mom I was going out for breakfast. Instead, I went to the airport, booked a flight, and here I am."

I stare at my sister, shocked. "You told Mom you were going out for breakfast and decided to casually take a plane to Montana?"

Scarlett bites her lip and shrugs.

"Just like me," Bellamy chimes in. "Well, sort of."

Behind me, Blake barks out a laugh.

It's then I remember my manners. Taking my sister's hand, I steer us toward where Blake and Bellamy are watching by the bar. Blake's sister is sitting on a stool, legs swinging while sipping on a soda, while Blake is standing with his hip propped against the bar and his arms crossed over his chest.

"Blake, Bellamy, this is my baby sister, Scarlett."

"Hi!" Bellamy gives my sister a pleasant wave while Blake offers her a chin lift.

"How's it goin'?"

Scarlett leans in close and whispers, "Is that him? He's..." She looks at Blake and then back at me. "Big." She's still whispering.

Having heard what Scarlett said, Bellamy giggles. Blake looks unaffected, but I don't miss the twitch of his lip.

I look at my sister to see a red tint staining her cheeks. I nudge her with my elbow. "Wait here a second while I talk to Blake."

I gesture for Blake to follow me into the kitchen out of earshot. He quickly ensures I'm okay by wrapping his arms around me. I lay my head against his chest, close my eyes and breathe in his scent. "My sister coming here will cause trouble with my parents."

"Your folks aren't going to do shit," Blake assures me.

"You don't know my parents."

"Don't give a fuck." Blake takes my face between the palms of his hands. "They can't touch you here. And they can't touch her, as long as your sister is here."

I close my eyes and sigh. "You're right."

"Are you going to be good, or do you want me to stay?"

I shake my head. "No. You and Bellamy go on. I want to catch up with my sister." I smile. "I still can't believe she's here. It's been so long."

Blake's face softens. "I'm happy for you, Vita Mia."

"Thanks." I go up on my tiptoes and kiss him. "We'll be fine."

"All right, baby. Grey is back if you need anything, and I'll have my cell."

Later that afternoon, Scarlett and I are sitting outside in the backyard of the clubhouse, drinking beer and catching up. She told me about school and how much she hates her classes.

"My offer still stands in sending you to design school," I remind her, taking a sip of beer.

"I accept."

Her calm reply takes me off guard, making me choke and sputter through my drink. "Really?" I snatch up a napkin and wipe my mouth.

"I accept your offer. I want to move here and go to design school."

Setting the bottle down on the table, I turn toward my sister. "Are you serious?" I try not to get my hopes up, but the thought of Scarlett moving here and being close to me full-time has me in a near tizzy.

"Please don't play with my emotions, Scar. My heart can't take it."

She slaps my arm. "I'm not. I'm being serious. I'm done with Mom and Dad controlling me, and I'm done with their high expectations." She picks at the label on the bottle in her hand. "I want to start living life for me and do what makes me happy." Scarlett sets her drink down. "Being with my sister and attending design school will make me happy."

"Come here." I pull my baby sister into my arms.

"You know Mom and Dad are going to shit a brick when they find out where I am."

"Yeah, but I don't care. Let them."

Scarlett pulls back. "You also know there's a good chance they'll cause trouble."

I grin. "I don't care about that, either. The club has my back and yours too."

"Speaking of." She looks around the yard like she's waiting for a bunch of bikers to pop out from behind the bushes. "Where are all these people you talk my ear off about?"

I look down at my watch. "Blake will be back soon, and you'll meet everyone else shortly. I already called Jake and told him you were here, and he said Grace is itching to meet you but he told her to give us some time to ourselves."

"Grace; is she Jake's wife?"

"Yes, and Jake is the club's President."

Scarlett looks thoughtful and asks, "Who was the one caught naked with a stethoscope around his neck?"

"That would be Quinn." A deep voice answers as Grey steps into view, making my sister jump. "Sorry, didn't mean to scare ya," he tells her. "I just came to let you know Blake will be late. Bellamy roped him into stopping by the mall. He tried calling, but you didn't answer."

"Oh." I look around for my phone but come up empty. "I must have left it on my desk."

"No worries. I told him all was good here." Grey jerks his head. "Holler if you two need anything."

"Thanks, Grey."

Once Grey disappears around the corner, Scarlett asks, "Who is he with? Is he married?"

"Nope. Not married. But he is sweet about Emma, the town librarian and friend of the club."

"Why aren't they together? Does she not like him back?"

"She definitely likes him back. She's just...hesitant, I think. What about you?" I steer the conversation.

"What about me?"

I roll my eyes. "Don't play dumb. What's going on with you and Keith? Does he know you're here?"

Scarlett sighs. "No. We fought before I left school. He didn't want me to go back to Mom and Dad. He begged me to stay. He even asked me to move in with him, saying he'd take care of me and pay for whatever school I wanted to go to."

"And you said no?" I raise my brow.

Scarlett nods. "I couldn't take the chance of Mom and Dad finding out and doing everything in their power to make his life hell. They wouldn't accept him, Em. You know it." Scarlett looks off in the distance and grows quiet. "I'm pretty sure I screwed things up with him. I'm miserable, Em."

"Scar." I reach out and grab her hand.

Scarlett wipes away a tear from her cheek. "I admire your strength and am jealous that you had the guts to break free years ago."

"You're strong too, Scarlett."

"I'm weak."

"You're not weak. Look at you. Look at where you're sitting."

A ghost of a smile crosses her face. "I'm happy I'm here, Em."

"I'm happy you're here too. I love you, Scarlett."

The next day, I'm in the kitchen with Lisa and Raine, trying to help with food prep, when Lisa shoos me out of the way. "Go on. Out of the kitchen. Let's go."

"I'm just trying—"

Lisa cuts me off. "I know what you're doing, and I'm not having any of it."

"You better listen to her, Ember." Raine smirks.

"Fine," I huff. "I'm going."

"Here." Lisa passes me a platter of freshly-baked chocolate chip cookies. "Take this with you. The cookies should hold the kids at bay until dinner is made. Just make sure Quinn doesn't see them."

I laugh. "Fat chance."

Lisa looks thoughtful. "You're right. Give him this." She walks over to the refrigerator and rummages around until she finds what she's looking for; a container of last night's leftover spaghetti and meatballs.

"Shouldn't you warm it up first?" Raine asks.

"He won't care," Lisa tosses out.

I do as I'm told and return to where the club has gathered for a cookout. Jake, Grace, Logan, and Bella showed up early this morning and announced they were bringing the whole family together. Jake figured with both Blake's and my sisters showing up, it was the perfect way to welcome them and for everyone to get to know each other. By noon the whole clan had arrived, including Demetri and Glory. I, of course, did what I always do when we have the club together, which is to help with the cooking. But I was given strict orders from Jake and Lisa to spend the day with my sister.

"Need some help, baby?" Blake takes the platter of cookies from my hand. Like they have a sugar radar, several kids cheer as they come barreling toward us. One of the first kids to reach us is Gabe, Alba's little boy. He reaches out, snatching up four cookies while the rest of the brood nearly bring Blake down as little hands wrestle for their take. I watch Gabe trek across the lawn to the swing set, where his little sister waits patiently with a huge smile. Then I witness him handing over three cookies to Val, keeping one for himself.

My attention shifts away from the kids when I spot Quinn striding this way, rubbing his hands together. "Are there any cookies left for me?"

"Sorry, brother," Blake offers. "The rugrats beat ya to them."

"What?" Quinn looks crestfallen. "That's not fair." He starts looking around the yard. His gaze lands on Jake and Bella, with Logan's son sitting on top of one of the picnic tables, holding a stack of cookies. I cover my mouth to hide my smile because I know what Jake is doing, and so does Quinn. "Dammit. He does this every time."

Blake slaps Quinn on the shoulder. "Don't hate the player, brother. Hate the game."

"Yeah, well, the player made me pay him five bucks last week for the last brownie. His prices have been increasing," he grumbles.

"Well, I don't have any cookies, but here." I hand Quinn the container of cold spaghetti I've been holding, and he eagerly takes it from me and pops the lid. Fork in hand, he begins shoveling the spaghetti into his mouth.

"Damn, Quinn." Blake looks disgusted. "You're not going to heat that shit first?"

Quinn pauses, looking thoughtful, then shrugs. "If you two will excuse me, I need to see a man about some cookies."

"There is seriously something wrong with him," I giggle.

Later that evening, we all gather around the fire after filling our bellies with good food. I'm sitting on Blake's lap, my head on his chest, listening to the low rumble of conversation around me as my eyes grow heavy. I watch Austin step behind Jake and mutter something close to his ear, and Jake's attention becomes alert.

The conversation halts, and all eyes are now on Jake, who taps Grace's leg, a signal for her to get up from where she's perched on his lap, a worried look on her face.

No longer feeling sleepy, I stand, and Blake follows. "What is it, Prez?" he asks.

"Austin says there is a man and woman at the gate." Jake looks at Blake. "They say they're here to pick up their daughter."

My first thought is someone has come for Bellamy. I reach out to Blake, who says, "That is not fuckin' happenin', Prez."

"Baby, get the kids inside," Jake tells Grace, then jerks his chin at Blake. "Let's go."

Blake falls in beside Jake, and the other men quickly follow suit.

Scarlett rushes up to me. "What's going on?"

"I'm not sure, but I think it has something to do with Bellamy."

"You don't think Blake will let them take her, do you?" Raine asks.

"No way." I start walking across the yard in the direction the guys just disappeared. My sister, Raine, Bella, and Mila tag along. Before I even round the corner of the clubhouse, I instantly recognize a raised male voice. I stop and look at Scarlett, and her face pales. "Dad," she whispers.

"Shit," I hiss, and take off in a jog with my sister hot on my heels. When I reach the compound's entrance, all I see is a wall of muscle. Standing between Jake and Logan, Blake sees me and looks over his shoulder at me. "Get inside, baby."

"Stay with Bella," I tell Scarlett. Ignoring Blake, I make my approach.

"I demand to see my daughter," my father barks.

"I don't give a fuck how things work where you're from, but

you're standin' on Kings territory, and that means you don't make demands," Blake snarls.

I reach the wall of men standing between my parents and me and push my way between Blake and Logan, coming face-to-face with two people I haven't seen in years. Nothing about them has changed. My father sports a perfectly tailored navy suit with gold cufflinks and perfectly cut hair. My mom is in one of her signature cream pantsuits, a scarf around her neck, a simple string of pearls, and, as usual, not a strand of hair out of place. My mother barely contains her gasp of surprise but quickly recovers. My father, however, looks at me with disgust. "Where is she?"

I cross my arms over my chest and pop my hip. "Nice to see you too, Dad." There is no mistaking the sarcastic tone of my greeting.

"Don't get cute with me, you little tramp." My father points his finger at my face. Behind me is a scuffle, and from the corner of my eye, I see Gabriel and Logan holding Blake. My mother pales and inches closer to my father's side.

Jake straightens to his full height and takes a step forward. "Because you're Ember's father, I'll give you that one, but you get out of line one more time, and you'll regret the day you stepped your pompous ass onto my property," Jake warns, his tone lethal.

"You think I'm scared of you and your pack of criminals?" My dad lifts his nose in the air. "I'll have the police down here so fast your head will spin."

My father's sad threat earns him a chuckle from Logan, making my dad's face turn ten shades of red. Ignoring Jake's warning, my father turns his attention back to me. "I want to see my daughter."

"She doesn't want to see you."

"That's ludicrous," my mother chimes in. "You've probably gotten inside her head, filling it with nonsense."

"Ember is not filling my head with anything." Scarlett appears beside me.

My mother perks up at my sister's arrival. "Scarlett, honey, we've come to take you home."

"I'm not going home with you."

"Scarlett, listen to your mother. Retrieve your things, and we'll leave."

My sister grabs my hand, needing support, and I gently squeeze it.

"I'm staying here with Ember and dropping out of school. I've also been seeing someone. His name is Keith. He's a mechanic, and I'm in love with him," she exclaims all in one breath.

My father goes silent, and I can hear him grinding his molars. He narrows his hardened eyes at me. "This is why we have fought so hard to keep your sister from you. We knew you'd ruin her if you ever got your hooks into her. You ruin everything you touch. Look at Scarlett. She's dropped out of school and hooked up with some mechanic we know nothing about, and now we find her staying here, in this place, with you and a bunch of low-life criminals. You couldn't hack being a part of a respectable family. Instead, you brought us nothing but shame. You are not my daughter. You are nothing."

"Dad!" Scarlett gasps.

I stand there feeling empty inside as my flesh and blood spews his disdain for me. I refuse to let him see how badly his words hurt, but it takes all my strength to hold back the tears.

"What's next? Will you rub some more of that filth off on your sister? Will you turn your sister into a whore, just like you?"

15

BLAKE

Bone and cartilage crack against my knuckles, and Ember's father falls to his knees, his hand cupping his nose. Blood seeps between his fingers.

"Oh, my God!" Ember's mother cries as she reaches for her husband, but he rejects her help, pushing her away.

"You broke my goddamn nose." He spits, getting to his feet. "You have no idea who I am or what I can do to people like you."

"You're lucky busting your nose was all I did." I advance in his direction, and he stumbles back. I reach out and fist his shirt, slamming him against the chain link fence. "And you are sorely mistaken if you believe I give two shits who you are, motherfucker." I shove him one more time. "You and your uppity wife trespassed on our property. You have no power out here."

Ember's father takes a small white handkerchief from his suit pocket and presses it against his bent nose. "I'll have you brought up on assault charges and put in jail." He looks at his wife. "Call the local authorities."

I pull out my phone and smack it against his chest. "You do

that," I dare him, rage sweeping through me like wildfire. "By the time they arrive, it'll be too late." A look of fear blooms across his face, his eyes growing round.

Ember's mother gasps. "How dare you threaten my husband!"

I keep my eyes fixed on the bastard in front of me. "You are not welcome here. If you ever disrespect my woman in my presence again, I'll make you wish for death." I get right in his face. "And in case you don't get my meaning; if you ever cause Ember to shed one more tear, I'll have you digging your grave before I put a bullet in your head." Glaring at him, I watch my promise take root, then I release my hold on the piece of shit and back away. Ember comes to stand at my side, her hand slipping into mine.

Her mother shuffles toward her husband, trying to tend to him, but he brushes her touch off, his lip curling in a disdainful sneer. "This isn't over."

"This motherfucker isn't too bright, is he?" Gabriel huffs.

"Get the fuck off my property," Jake booms, his voice laced with annoyance, "and get the hell out of Polson." Jake looks over at Gabriel. "See to it they do."

"You've made your choice." Ember's father glares at her, and she grabs my hand tighter.

"You're damn right I have." She straightens her back and holds her head high.

Her dad cuts his eyes to Scarlett, standing close to Ember's other side. "If you stay, don't bother coming home again." His words cause Ember and Scarlett's mother's face to fall.

"I'm staying." Scarlett stands her ground.

Their father's face tightens, and his nostrils flare, but he doesn't utter another word. Gabriel strolls over to Ember's parents, looming over them. "Move it," he growls, and sees them off the property.

I turn, facing Ember, and embrace her. She melts into me,

burying her face in my chest. The emotions she was keeping at bay become too abundant to hold in. Her shoulders tremble, and she begins to cry, her tears dampening the front of my shirt. I spread my arms, welcoming Scarlett into my embrace, too, and hold both women as they cry.

16

EMBER

It's been two days since the blowup with my parents. My sister and I expected them to cause a problem, but never in a million years thought they'd show up at the clubhouse. However, I did get a sick satisfaction seeing Blake hit my father. Yet Dad's words continue to play on repeat inside my head. Every time I remember the disgust on his face and the venom-laced words that spewed from his mouth, a piece of my heart chips away. Because no matter how long I have been estranged from my parents and how unhappy I was living at home, I still love them. I'm angry at myself for just standing there and allowing my dad to say everything he did. I'm even more furious for allowing myself to believe them. I can't control what others say or do, but I can control how I react. At that moment, my father managed to hold all the power. The bitter taste of jealousy found its way inside, causing my stomach to knot at the fact that my parents flew across the country for my sister, but they had not once done that for me. When I decided not to return home, no one showed up at my doorstep to fight for me. Am I that disposable? Am I not worth fighting for? These are just a couple of the thoughts that have been plaguing me.

Sure, on the outside, it looks as though I don't give a shit, but the battle I'm fighting on the inside is real. Words hold power, and they sometimes knock down even the strongest people. Especially when the ones wielding those insults are the people who are supposed to love you unconditionally. Too bad my parents' love comes with conditions. Never mind being happy. To them, life is keeping up with the Joneses. God forbid you go off script. Why can't they be glad I'm happy?

"Baby." Blake's raspy voice pulls me out of my inner turmoil. I look over at the bed where he's been asleep for the past few hours. "It's four-thirty in the mornin'. What are you still doing up?"

"I couldn't sleep, so I thought I'd crank some words out," I lie. The words aren't coming, and I've been staring at the blank computer screen for hours.

Blake studies me momentarily, and I can tell he knows I'm lying. Luckily, he doesn't call me out on it. The last thing I want is to talk about my parents again. My sister means well, but she constantly asks if I'm okay or want to talk. Same with Bella, since she was there to witness the showdown. Jake pulled me aside not long after they kicked my parents off the compound to ensure I was okay too. I'm thankful Blake senses my mood and knows me well enough not to push. Instead, he climbs out of bed, picks his clothes up from the floor, and gets dressed. Striding over to where I'm sitting, he kisses me. "Get dressed and meet me outside."

On his way out, he grabs his cut and snatches his keys and phone off the top of the dresser. I stare at his back as he leaves. I'm left confused, but I shake it off and do what I'm told. Walking to my closet, I grab a pair of black jeans, a tank top, and a purple flannel. Once I'm dressed, I step into a pair of boots.

When I leave the clubhouse, I find Blake straddling his bike with a cigarette hanging from his mouth. His eyes never leave me as I make my way toward him. "Where are we going?" I ask. Instead of answering me, he passes me a helmet. Wordlessly, I take it from his grip and secure it on my head before climbing on the bike behind him. Neither of us says a word as he fires up the engine. I slide my arms around his waist as he peels through the open gate of the compound. We pass by Grey, who jerks his chin when Blake tosses up a one-finger salute.

At four o'clock in the morning, the streets of Polson are still empty. Blake hits the main road, and we pass by Kings Custom. Making a right turn, we soon pass the bakery. We clear the city limits and make our way up the mountain. The temperature drops the farther up we go. With the moon lighting our way, we ride the winding roads, and a sense of calmness settles through me. Before I know it, the tension I was feeling melts away. Soon the smell of fresh, crisp air caresses my face. Then it hits me. Blake knew I didn't want to talk, but he knew I needed an escape. Since moving to Polson, my favorite place to be has always been the mountains. I could spend hours driving up here with the windows down and my hair blowing in the breeze. Now, my favorite place to be is riding the mountain roads on the back of Blake's bike. Leaning forward, I kiss the nape of his neck.

The sun rises over the mountain when we reach my favorite lookout spot. Parking the bike, Blake climbs off, faces me, and straddles the bike once more. He then grabs my legs and drapes them over his thighs, bringing my center flush against his. I smile at him. "Don't you want to watch the sunrise?"

"Yes."

"You're facing the wrong way."

"No, I'm not."

"But you're looking at me."

"I want to watch the sun rise in your eyes, Vita Mia."

My breath catches in my throat, leaving me speechless. With nothing left to say, I watch the sun peek over the mountain's top, bringing a new day with new possibilities.

17

BLAKE

Ember moans as I move to get out of bed. She drapes her leg over my hip, clamping on. "Mmm. Stay just a little longer," she mumbles, half asleep.

I chuckle and kiss the top of her head. "Sorry, babe. We ride before dawn." I slide from beneath her, instantly missing the heat of her naked body against mine, and stroll into the bathroom. I flip the light on, stand in front of the sink, and splash cold water on my face a few times. I'm staring at my reflection when thin arms wrap around my middle from behind.

"Talk to me," she pleads. "I know this trip has you stressed. Does it have something to do with Bellamy?"

I spin around and lift her onto the counter, stepping between her thighs. She rests her forehead against my chest. "You know I can't talk about club business, babe." I rest my chin on her head, run my palms up and down her thighs, and close my eyes.

Ember sighs and the warmth of her breath brushes my skin. "I know. It's just that I can't shake this feeling that something will happen."

I gently touch her chin. "Look at me." I wait for her to make eye contact. "Danger comes with the patch, baby. Taking all steps necessary to keep our families safe comes with risks we're all willing to take."

"Just make sure you come back to me."

"Nothing will keep me from returning home to you." I grip her hips, pulling her closer to where I feel the heat of her center against me. "I've got a long-ass ride ahead of me, so kiss me, Vita Mia. And make it good."

We're several hours into our road trip, and my ass is feeling it. We've been pushing through, only stopping to fill tanks and drain lizards every two hours. Jake tosses his hand, signaling to pull into the gas station ahead. At the same time, three riders pass, heading in the opposite direction, too fast for me to catch if they're wearing any colors.

We bring our bikes to a stop beside the gas pumps, and I look back in the direction the three bikers are headed. "Anyone catch their colors?" A chorus of *no* follows up my question.

"Could be weekend riders," Quinn says. "Everyone knows the drill. If you have to hit the head, do it now. This is our last stop before reaching the Utah-Nevada border." Finished filling his tank with gas, he strolls inside.

I finish topping off my tank, pull out my phone, and text Ember.

Me: Everyone good?

Her reply comes through instantly.

Ember: Yep. We're all piled up in the common room, watching a movie waiting for Grey to return with pizza.

My stomach rumbles with hunger at the mention of food, so I walk inside the gas station to use the restroom and buy a quick snack to shovel down my throat.

Me: Got to go.

Ember: Stay safe.

Me: Always.

I shove the phone back into my pocket and tend to business. Everyone is ready to hit the road when I return to my bike.

"Listen up," Jake barks. "We have roughly two more hours of ride time before reaching our destination. Remain vigilant of our surroundings. Any signs of Satan's Hounds outside of the agreed-upon neutral location are considered a threat, and we will act accordingly." He throws his leg over the seat of his Harley. "Roll out."

Time slows to a crawl on the last leg of the road trip. The closer we get to the border, the heavier my body feels. I always knew the day would come when I would have to face my past. My priority is the club's and my family's safety, including Bellamy's. I won't let her return to the hell she lived in before; nor will the club. My uncle has been keeping tabs on me, but the question is why, and for how long? What is their motive? Do they know Bellamy found her way to Polson? And if so, why haven't they attempted to bring her home? Was this all a setup and they're using my sister to get to me?

I take a deep breath and try to clear the rampant invasive thoughts in my head. Not that they don't hold validity, but I don't need the distraction. My head needs to be in the present. I need to focus on having my brothers' backs and protecting the club. I need to lay the past to rest once and for all, so I can move forward and build a life for Ember and myself without looking over my shoulder all the damn time.

Once we reach the Utah-Nevada border, we exit the highway. We take a frontage road, riding another several miles until a rundown motel comes into view. Across the street is a rundown brick building with a sign that reads Dirty D's, which has half-a-dozen vehicles parked in the dirt field adjacent to it. We pull into the parking lot riddled with potholes. Across from the office is an unclean pool filled with brownish-green stagnant water, which explains the pungent smell of rotten eggs. Logan dismounts his bike and strolls inside the office. A few minutes later, he returns with one key, twirling it around his finger. "Our room is twenty-seven, down on the end."

"You mean to tell me all five of us are sharin' a room?" Quinn stays seated on his bike.

"No bitchin'," Jake fires back. "We're in unfamiliar territory. Safety first, which means we're bunkin' together on this one." He revs his engine, rolls his bike back across the narrow parking lot toward the end of the building, and backs his Harley in front of room twenty-seven. Grumbling, the rest of us follow suit.

Logan unlocks the door, and we file inside. A stale, musty odor greets us. The room is small, and the dark wood-paneled walls make the space feel more cramped. Overhead, the dingy white ceiling is tinged with tobacco smoke residue. There are two double beds with a small nightstand in between, covered in a thin layer of dust. I walk over and part the curtains, peering outside, but the window has a hazy layer of filth coating it. It barely lets any light in. The place is a shithole, but we've stayed in worse conditions. Jake moves one of the two chairs in the room close to the window, a few feet from the door, and sits. "Rest up. The sit-down doesn't take place until 10:00 pm."

With nothing more to do, we wait.

We're currently sitting inside Dirty Ds. It's a dingy, dimly lit hole-in-the-wall dive bar that smells of beer and stale cigarette smoke. Near the entrance, along the wall is the bar counter lined with wooden stools. With rolled-up sleeves, the guy tending the bar moves from one end of the counter to the other, wiping the surface clean. His eyes keep cutting in our direction, suspicious of our presence, but his attention doesn't linger. In the farthest corner of the bar room, a nude redhead with big tits begins her third set, working the pole, dancing to Buckcherry's Crazy Bitch.

The air in the room feels heavy, almost like the walls are closing in around me as the five of us sit silently at a table, backs against the wall, facing the bar's entrance and waiting. The music and murmurs of the other patrons soon fade into the background as I focus on the front door.

A few minutes later, the door swings open, and five men walk in. All the air is squeezed from my lungs as I set my eyes on one man in particular. His ice-cold stare lands on me. Aside from his dark hair turning gray, my uncle's appearance hasn't changed. He and his men weave around the scattered tables on their way toward the end of the bar where we're sitting. I push my chair from the table and stand, followed by Gabriel, Logan, and Quinn doing the same. Jake remains seated as the four of us flank his sides.

Hellhound stands around the same height as me but is much broader through the shoulders. "It's like seeing my brother's motherfuckin' ghost." One of his men snatches a chair from a nearby table and hands it to my uncle, who spins it around and straddles the seat. "So, you're in bed with another club." He cocks his head. "Where is your loyalty to the blood that runs through your veins?" he sneers, his face twisted with disdain.

"We may share the same blood, but that doesn't make you family, motherfucker. My loyalty is to the men beside me." I sense rage surging in his chest.

"We'll see." My uncle smirks, then shifts his attention to Jake.

Jake gets down to business. "You've been watching my club. Why?"

"My club always kept tabs on Blake when he was younger, making sure he kept his mouth shut. But, you see, Blake vanished around the same time my brother was found with a bullet in his head, and we lost track of his whereabouts, until now." He eyes me then shifts his attention back to Jake.

"What do you want?" Jake's tone turns lethal.

"For starters, I want the young woman you currently have in your possession."

"Over my dead body," I growl, swallowing the festering ball of fury. One of his men reaches into his leather cut, setting off a chain reaction. Chairs screech across the wood floor as the bar empties, leaving us the only people inside the building. The air thickens as each man stares down the barrel of another biker's gun.

"The bitch's whore mother gave her as payment. She is ours, motherfucker."

My finger itches to pull the trigger. "I'll put a bullet in your head before you ever get the chance to lay one finger on my sister, you cock-sucking bastard."

My uncle ignores my threat to his man. "The way I see it, you have no other options here. Bellamy stole from us. She owes me." My uncle narrows his eyes to slits and shoots daggers at me. "And so do you."

Jake hardens his face. "The Kings don't owe you shit."

"Oh, but you do. Because I believe you also have two of my men in your possession."

His men? Then it dawns on me. The bastards who broke into the garage and bakery are my uncle's men. Those were the motherfuckers spying on me and the club.

There's a beat of silence before Jake fires back, "You stick your nose where it doesn't belong, you pay the price. They stole from my club. Your men are dead."

My uncle lights a cigarette. "I thought as much." His features turn to stone, his eyes becoming a darker shade of black. He exhales, blowing smoke from his lungs. "Consider their deaths my payment. I'm only here for the girl." He cuts his eyes back toward me, and the motherfucker grins. "After all, sharing the same blood doesn't make you family, so handing her over shouldn't be too hard." He throws my words back in my face, and my anger erupts.

Before I move, a large hand clamps down on my shoulder. "Now is not the time," Gabriel warns.

Hellhound stands, looking down at Jake. "I'll tell you what. I'm a gracious man." He jabs the cigarette against the surface of the table, snuffing it out. "You've got one week to hand her over."

Jake rises to his full height, a couple inches taller than my uncle. "You'll be waiting for a long time, motherfucker. The Kings don't do ultimatums."

My uncle's lips thin, and he snaps his fingers. Turning on his heel, he walks away, his men backstepping, keeping their weapons raised as they exit the bar. It's only when the sound of their bikes fades that we holster our weapons.

"What's our next move?" Quinn asks.

With a fiery wrath, Jake claims, "We prepare for war."

18

EMBER

It's late afternoon, after my sister hit me up to go shopping earlier in the day. Blake and the men have been gone since yesterday, dealing with club business, but are expected to return home today. So, with permission to leave the compound, Scarlett and I headed into town.

Scarlett left most of her stuff back in Georgia and needed clothes and other necessities. We also had to stop and get her a new cell, since our parents cut her off. They also froze her credit cards, and she no longer has access to her bank account, which had my father's name attached. Because she had been attending school full-time, she didn't have a job and was entirely dependent on our parents. Earlier, Scarlett tried to put up a fight about the phone and me adding her to my account. Now she is currently having a fit at the electronic store. I didn't tell her ahead of time we were coming because I knew how she'd react when I told her I would be buying her a new laptop and a tablet. After doing some research on what is the best tablet for design, I pick her the recommended one.

"Em, this is too much." Scarlett tries to take the laptop and tablet from me as we arrive at the checkout.

I casually slap her hand out of the way. "It's not too much. Besides, you'll need this stuff for school."

"I can just borrow your computer when I need it."

"Nope. You'll have your own."

"Damnit, Ember." She stomps her foot.

"Stop being a brat, Scar."

Scarlett crosses her arms over her chest and pouts. "I'm not being a brat."

I side-eye her with a raised brow. "Mmhm."

"Whatever." She rolls her eyes.

When we get to the register and she sees the total, her eyes bug out.

"Relax." I pull out my credit card and swipe it through the card reader.

"I'm going to pay you back every penny, Em. I promise," my baby sister says as we make our way out of the store.

"No, you won't," I counter.

"You're so damn bossy," she grumbles, making me laugh.

"Yeah, well, get used to it. That's what big sisters are for: to boss their little sisters around."

"Is that so?"

I bump Scarlett's shoulder. "Yep. Those are the rules."

She links her arm with mine. "Thank you, Em."

"You're welcome."

As we approach my car, I notice the woman parked beside me struggling to get a baby stroller into the back of her vehicle. The closer we get, the better I see why. Her left arm is in a cast. "Need some help?" I rush to offer my assistance.

The woman looks frazzled but still offers a warm smile. "Oh, thank you so much. It's not easy maneuvering this thing with one hand." She holds up her casted arm.

"I can see that." I grip the closing mechanism on either side of the stroller and pull back, folding it in half. I'm just about to lift in into the back of her car when the sound of screeching tires catches my attention. I whip around to see a white van come to a halt right in front of us. The side door slides open, and three men jump out. Moving into action, I turn to grab my sister but stop short when I see the lady I was just helping holding a gun to my sister's head. She smirks. "Night, night." Then she brings the butt of the gun down on Scarlett's temple. I don't have time to react, because a second later, everything goes black.

I wake up some time later, disoriented and encased in darkness. For a moment, I think I'm waking from a dream, until I become aware of a dull throb at the base of my skull. Confusion sets in, because my eyes are open, yet darkness surrounds me. I try to move, but something is holding me in place. Then I realize my wrists are bound behind my back, and I'm sitting upright on a hard surface. Something is covering my head, and I panic. I try to fight against my restraints, but the ropes tied around my wrists and ankles rub painfully against my skin. I cry out in pain when I feel my flesh tear, and something wet seeps down my palm.

"Ember?" I hear my name being called, but it sounds muffled.

"Scarlett? Are you there?"

"Oh my god, Ember," she chokes out. "What's going on? I can't see, and I can't move." My sister's words come out in a panic. "My head hurts," she sobs.

"It's going to be okay. Scarlett."

"It's not going to be okay!" my sister cries. "Someone kidnapped us, Ember! Who were those men? What do they want?"

"I don't know, but I need you to calm down, okay?"

Scarlett continues to sob. "We're going to die. I don't want to die."

"You're not going to die, Scarlett. I won't let that happen." The lie rolls off my tongue, causing a knot of dread to form in the pit of my stomach. The truth is, I don't know what's going to happen or what is going on.

"Scarlett, listen to me. Someone had to have seen something and called the police. Grey, Reid, and Austin will expect us back at the clubhouse. When we don't show, they'll go looking for us." This time I don't lie. Blake has been texting every few hours to keep tabs on everyone. When I don't answer, he'll worry. It will take him only a short time to figure out something isn't right.

"Ember," Scarlett wheezes. "I can't breathe." Her breaths come out in heavy pants as she starts to hyperventilate.

"Listen to me, Scarlett. Slow your breathing down."

"I can't," she rasps, "breathe."

"Yes, you can. Now concentrate on my voice. Slow, steady breaths. In through your nose and out your mouth. Come on. Again." We do this several more times together before I hear her breathing even back out. "That's good, Scarlett. You're going to be okay."

"Do...do you really believe that?" Her question comes out shakily.

I want desperately to keep reassuring my sister everything will be okay, but the truth is, I'm not so sure. I believe in Blake and the club and in them finding us. I'm about to tell my sister when heavy footsteps are followed by a scraping sound. "Look at what we have here, boys."

I begin to thrash from side to side and try again to free my wrists.

"We have a wildcat on our hands," someone chuckles.

Suddenly, the covering over my head rips off, and I'm blinded by a bright light, causing my eyes to water. Once my vision adjusts, I ignore the three men standing before me and seek out Scarlett. She's about ten feet away, tied to a metal chair like I am, with a black hood over her head. Even from where I sit, I can see her body tremble with fear and her chest's rapid rise and fall. One of the guys jerks his chin and orders his friend to remove the hood over her head. She cries out as the light blinds her. I wait for her to find me, and when she does, her eyes widen. "Ember!"

"It's okay, Scar."

My sister starts to cry even harder. "Let us go! Please!" She tries to wiggle free from the rope bound at her wrists.

"Don't worry. We're going to let you go." I watch a large man with a greasy ponytail tied at the nape of his neck stalk toward Scarlett. "Not before we have a little fun first." Then, without warning, he backhands her across the face.

"*Leave her alone, you piece of shit!*" I scream. Bile rises in my throat when blood trickles from the cut on her lip. My sister has never been hit before, and here she is, having this vile man put his hands on her. "You're dead," I seethe.

My threat has the three men roaring with laughter. "Yeah, what are you going to do? It looks like you're in no position to be makin' threats."

"Fuck you, asshole."

I don't see the first strike coming; I only feel immense pain radiating across my cheek. Before I can recover, another blow strikes my face. This time, my vision blurs around the edges. Large hands wrap around my throat, constricting my windpipe. Pressure builds behind my eyes as I thrash, fighting to breathe. Just before I black out, I'm gasping, sucking air into my lungs. Laughter, mixed with sobs, fills the space around me. "Scarlett." I take another shuddered breath and lift my head to look at her. Unfortunately, another round of brutality begins before I can make eye contact.

I hear someone calling my name, but it's muffled, with a slight echo like I'm in a tunnel. It takes all my strength to force my eyes open, and my vision is blurry as I try to make out the figure leaning over me.

"Oh god, Ember. You have to wake up. Please wake up."

"Scarlett?" I groan.

"Yes, Em, it's me. We have to get out of here before they come back."

"Before who..." I begin to ask when, like a freight train, my memory comes flooding back. Scarlett and me shopping. The lady with the stroller. Being taken. That man hitting Scarlett. Then that same man beating me. "Scarlett!" I shoot straight up and immediately regret it when I'm suddenly overcome with extreme nausea. Vomit rises in my throat, and without warning, I lean over and release the entire contents of my stomach onto the dirty concrete floor.

Beside me, my sister is sobbing. "Ember, what do I do? We need to get you to the hospital."

Wiping my mouth with the back of my hand, I ignore the pounding inside my head and how every inch of my body screams in pain. "How long was I out? And when did they leave?"

"I don't know. Maybe thirty minutes." Scarlett sniffles. "Can you stand?"

"I think so. I need you to help me up." I grab Scarlett's hand. Taking a deep breath, I fight nausea and dizziness to get my feet underneath me. My sister bears as much weight as she can to help me stand, and I grit my teeth against the pain in my ribs. "How did you get loose?" I ask.

"One of those assholes cut my hands free before they left. I worked my legs free, then helped you. Oh, God, Em, I thought you were dead," she sobs. "They were hurting you so bad. They just kept on hitting. I didn't think they'd ever stop." She wraps her arms around me.

"I'm so sorry I got you into this," I tell her. "But don't worry. We're going to get out of here." I look around the empty warehouse. "Let's go." Scarlett and I make our way outside. The parking lot is vacant, and I don't recognize the area. It's pitch black, aside from the blurry streetlight in the distance.

"Where are we?" my sister asks.

"I don't know." Another bout of dizziness washes over me. "Let's head in that direction." I point toward the light. If we can reach the main road, we can flag down some help.

"What if those guys show up?"

"They won't." If those men wanted us dead, we'd be dead. I make sure to keep that part to myself. What those men were doing was delivering a message. "Come on."

Slowly, Scarlett and I make our way through a field of overgrown brush. I know we're headed in the right direction when I spot the road a few yards ahead.

19

BLAKE

My head is throbbing, the pain radiating down my neck and spine. Every muscle in my body is locked with built-up tension. Ahead, Jake increases his speed, and I twist my throttle and follow suit with the others. We've been pushing ourselves since sunrise, racing to get home. We contemplated whether to turn right around and head back last night, but Jake decided to stay at the shitty motel room for safety, saying it was better to travel at daylight. We all tried to rest, but sleep evaded us.

The fact that it was no secret that my uncle's club knew our location also played a factor in our unrest. Seven days. It doesn't give us much time. And there's no knowing how Satan's Hounds will come at us when we don't meet their demand to hand over my sister. Bile rises in my throat, bitterness coating my tongue as my thoughts drift back to last night and the motherfucker staking his claim to Bellamy. She's a fucking kid. The sick fuck. I should have put a bullet in him right then and there. Everything about our current situation is new territory for the club. Not that the stakes haven't been high in past battles, but this time is different. We all know what lies ahead, that there is only one outcome to all of this.

I shudder to think what will happen to Bellamy should my uncle's club get a hold of her again.

My thoughts shift to Ember. We're less than an hour from hitting the Polson city limit sign, and all I can focus on is getting home. I texted her during our last pit stop, but she hasn't responded. I'm already keyed up after the previous night's sit-down, and my woman's lack of communication threatens to push me over the edge.

We blow past a small, abandoned industrial site, an indicator that we're closing in on Polson. Just a few miles more, and we'll be turning our bikes toward the direction of the clubhouse. A reflection in my side mirror catches my attention, and I give the distraction another glance. The fuck? Where the hell did they come from? Someone is in the middle of the road, arms waving. Shit. I can't ignore them. I slow my speed and turn the bike around.

The closer I get to the person, who has now moved to the side of the road, the more recognition sets in. It's Scarlett, and my heart sinks to my stomach. By this time, my brothers are closing in behind me as I come to a sudden stop.

"Oh, my God!" Scarlett stumbles, falling to her knees on her way toward me. She clings to my forearms as I lift her.

"Where's Ember?" My head races with frenzied, disjointed thoughts as she sobs uncontrollably. "Scarlett!" I shout, trying to snap her out of hysterics. She finally looks at me. *"Where is Ember?"*

Taking a deep, shuddering breath, Scarlett points toward the ditch. "She passed out again. They took our phones, everything. I didn't know what else to do but wait for someone to drive by and help."

My gaze catches on Ember's body, mostly hidden by the thick, overgrown grass, unmoving. "No." The air in my lungs leaves my body. Leaving Scarlett, I rush to Ember, falling to my knees. Her shirt is covered in blood, and her face is badly beaten. "Ember, baby." I brush blood-matted hair from her face.

"Jesus," Logan mutters, standing over me. "Is she breathin'?"

"She's alive," I announce.

"I'll call Reid and have him bring transportation," Quinn rushes out.

"That will take twice as long. We need to get her to Doc!" I yell back at Quinn but keep my eyes trained on Ember. "Talk to me, baby," I plead as my hands move across her body, looking for bullet or stab wounds. She moans as I roll her onto her side to assess her back for injury. Thankfully, I find none.

"Blake?" She blinks, cracking her swollen eyes open.

"I'm here, Vita Mia."

"Where's my sister?"

I look over my shoulder, spotting Scarlett being tended to by Jake, who is on the phone, most likely talking with Doc. "She's with Jake." I scoop Ember off the ground, carry her to my bike, and help her stand. Jake approaches me, leaving Scarlett with Quinn.

"Doc is waiting for us." His eyes rake over Ember, taking in her visible injuries, and the muscle in his jaw twitches. "Who did this to you?" Jake asks Ember.

She lifts her face to Jake, licking her lips coated with dried blood. "Three bikers with Satan's Hounds patches."

My blood runs cold. I glance at my brothers, and their expressions darken, knowing this is only the beginning of what is sure to come.

"We need to get the fuck out of here," Logan orders. "Now."

I look back at Ember. "Baby, I need you to get on the bike."

Ember nods. "Okay." With assistance, Ember climbs onto the seat. "I think I'm going to throw up." Just as the words come out of her mouth, Ember wretches. I hold her hair back as she empties the contents of her stomach. Using the front of my shirt to wipe her lips, I gently slip a helmet over her head, then climb on the bike.

Jake straps a helmet on Scarlett and places her on the back of his bike as the others mount their rides, gearing up to take off. "Tuck in as close as you can and wrap your arms around my middle, baby." I wait for her to do as I said. "Whatever you do, don't let go."

Ember presses her body against mine and whispers, "I knew you would come for me." Her arms squeeze against my ribcage as tight as she can get them.

"I always will," I promise, and pull onto the road, racing to get my woman and her sister to the safety of the clubhouse.

Dread settles in my stomach. While we sat across from those bastards, they sent men to Polson. A blazing inferno of red-hot rage blooms throughout my body, burning me from the inside out.

I will find the motherfuckers who dared to lay hands on my woman. When I do, their deaths will be slow and painful.

Austin is waiting at the gate as we approach the compound. Ember is weaker than before, so I carry her inside, taking her straight to her room with Doc and Emerson close behind. I lay her on the bed and step off to the side, giving Doc plenty of room to look her over. After a few minutes, Doc allows Emerson to take over. She sits on the side of the bed, holding Ember's hand. They're talking, but I can't hear what is said. Doc stands in front of me. "Let's take a walk, son."

"Why?"

"Emerson needs to examine Ember." It doesn't take long for me to realize why. I reluctantly walk out of the bedroom. I stare at the closed door, and my fists ball at my sides. "Her injuries are mainly isolated to her face and left rib cage, and nothing appears to be broken. I suspect she has a slight concussion, from her dizziness and nausea. Those bastards worked her over good." Doc sighs, and I can tell by how his expression changes that I won't like what he says next. "She doesn't recall any sexual assault, but she is aware that she was unconscious for an unknown amount of time, which is why Emerson wants to check her out."

The thought of her being...I can't even think of the word with my stomach coiling and my mouth going dry. Pacing the hall, my chest rising and falling with rapid breaths, I try tamping my emotions with no success. A few feet away, Doc keeps his distance. Several minutes pass, and the anger inside festers into a murderous rage.

The door opens, and Emerson steps into the hall. She looks at me. "Everything is okay." Relief washes over me, and I let out a heavy sigh. "She's asking for you."

I breeze past her and rush to Ember's side. She opens her swollen eyes when I take her hand in mine, and I swallow hard past the lump of emotions in my throat. Silence hangs between us as we stare at one another. Sometimes saying nothing at all is more powerful than words. Not letting loose of her hand, I slide into the bed and tuck her close to my side. Her hand rests on my chest over my heart, and she lays her head on my shoulder. Sometimes all we need is someone not to let go, and that's exactly what I give my woman while she quietly cries in my arms.

A short time later, Ember has fallen asleep, and there's a light rapping against the bedroom door just before it slowly opens. Quinn is standing in the doorway. "Prez is callin' Church." he says, his voice low.

"I'll stay with my sister." Scarlett squeezes past Quinn, stepping into the bedroom. She approaches the bed, her eyes landing on Ember. Tears pool in her eyes and her lower lip quivers as she tries to keep her emotions at bay.

I kiss Ember's forehead, slip from beneath her, and stop in front of Scarlett. "How you holdin' up?" She may have come out of this situation physically unscathed, but emotionally it's a lot to handle.

Scarlett closes her eyes and takes a deep breath. "I need my sister."

I nod in understanding, and Scarlett steps around me, slides in facing her sister, and holds her hand. Knowing my woman isn't alone helps me to leave the room, and I follow Quinn downstairs.

The rest of my brothers are in Church waiting when we walk inside. Too pent-up to sit still, I remain standing as the others sit.

"How's Ember?" Jake looks at me.

"Sleepin'."

"Good." He nods and adds, "How are you holdin' up?"

"I'll be better when I get my hands on the motherfuckers who hurt my woman." My tone is malicious with the desire to make them suffer.

Jake's phone rings, and he glances down at the table where it lies. He usually wouldn't take a call during Church, but he answers this time. "Yeah." He's silent for a beat. "Take him to the shed." Jake ends the call and cuts his eyes to me. "Looks like you're gettin' your wish."

Church is cut short, and we file out of the room. Most of the families are gathered in the common room, where the women have the kids gathered at tables eating an early dinner. The women eye us with concern but say nothing. "Doc, Austin, Sam, and Grey." Jake marches across the room. "Hold the fort down. No one comes in or out unless it's one of us or Demetri's men. The rest of you are with me," he barks, charging out the front door, and the rest of us follow him outside. "That was Demetri. Reid called in the favor after hearing about Satan's Hounds being involved with the kidnapping and assault on Ember and her sister. His men hit the roads, spotting the enemy heading south out of town. One of the men crashed his bike, and the others got away. Demetri should be arriving any minute with the remaining Satan's Hounds member," Jake explains as we trek across the property, making our way to the shed.

Moments later, we're standing around waiting for Demetri's arrival. I light a cigarette, inhale, feel the smoke enter my lungs, and hold it until my chest burns. Exhaling, I expel the smoke and nicotine my body didn't absorb, then repeat. No one talks, which is fine with me. I don't need anything else taking up my headspace. Right now, all I'm thinking about is inflicting unimaginable pain. A familiar black SUV approaches us, and behind it, a black sedan follows. They roll to a stop and the back door of the SUV opens. Demetri steps out, dressed in a tailored black suit, looking like he just walked out of a business meeting. Sasha walks to the back of the sedan as the men inside remain.

"Gentlemen." Demetri's steady gaze meets ours.

Jake approaches him and extends his hand, and the two shake. "Brother. Appreciate your help. Sticking around?"

"Wouldn't miss it." Demetri gets a familiar gleam in his eyes, and his pupils dilate. Death is looming, and he knows. Sasha drags a man from the car's trunk and shoves a gun to the back of the bastard's head. He says something to the asshole, but I don't understand Russian. He ushers a gagged Satan's Hounds member with his hands behind his back in our direction. He's older than I expected, maybe mid-fifties. The biker's stare connects with mine as he marches past. His eyes widen as if he's seen a ghost.

We file inside and close the barn doors. Gabriel shoves the cocksucker onto an empty high-back chair in the middle of the barn, securing his ankles to the chair legs and buckling a leather strap attached to the headrest across his forehead. My brothers and I form a semi-circle around our guest of honor. Gabriel rips away the gray tape covering the biker's lips and roughly pulls the cloth from inside his mouth, then backs away.

The man's lip curls, his eyes slit, sneering, "Do what you will, motherfuckers. I ain't talkin'." He spits on the ground.

"Whether you talk or not means nothin'." Jake crosses his arms over his chest. "You and your men kidnapped two of ours and put hands on my man's woman."

The dirty fucking Hound's head turns, his eyes latching onto mine. "She's a sweet piece of ass, too, for a whore. I should have shoved my cock down her throat and shown her what a real man tastes like." I clench my fists, and the cocksucker laughs. "Fucking coward. You may look like your old man but you are nothing like him."

That explains the way he looked at me before. I cut my eyes to Jake, who nods. I leave the semi-circle and tower over the bastard, producing a bone-handled hunting knife with a five-inch serrated blade. "You're right. I'm nothing like my father." I raise my hand and thrust the blade into his thigh. His screams feed my vengeful hunger, and I drag the embedded blade from the top of his thigh down to his knee, slicing his leg open.

"Goddamn. Fuck!" Spittle flies from the bastard's mouth. I don't give him time to take another gasping breath before repeating the same process on his other leg. "Argh! You. Mother. Fucking. Cock. Sucking. Bastard!" Blood soaks his lap, pooling in the seat and dripping onto the dirt floor.

"You tell us your club's next move; I just might end your pain and suffering," I lie, seeing if he's willing to give us something.

Color is slowly draining from the disgusting piece of shit's face as he loses blood. "Screw—" he breathes heavily "—you. You're all dead men." Laughter replaces his groaning.

I wipe the blood and flesh from my blade and put it back in the sheath, then take a pack of cigarettes from my pocket and offer the dying man a smoke. "One more before you die?" He says nothing as I place the filtered end between his chapped lips.

He spits it out. "Kill me and get it over with."

I ignore his request, place a cigarette between my lips, and pat my chest. "Anyone got a light?" I look around at my brothers.

Gabriel's lip twitches, and a sinister gleam lights in his eyes. He leaves the formation, returns with a handheld propane torch, and passes it to me. I ignite the torch and light the tip of my cigarette. With the torch still lit, I put the blue flame to the pussy's open wound. His screams reverberate off the barn walls. I turn off the torch and toss it to one of my brothers. We aren't here to interrogate the bastard. This torture session is for me—for the wrong done to Ember and her sister. Killing one of the Satan's Hounds responsible is retribution.

I draw my gun, pry the son of a bitch's mouth open, and shove the barrel down his throat, watching him choke on the metal. I pull the trigger, ending his worthless life. I back away, holster my weapon and look at Jake. "We done here?"

Jake nods. "Go be with your woman. We got it from here."

Once I return to the clubhouse, I enter through the kitchen, bypassing the women and children, not wanting them to see the blood-spatter on my shirt. I descend to the basement, removing my cut and tossing my shirt straight into the washing machine. I walk back out and climb directly up to Ember's bedroom. She and Scarlett are lying in bed awake when I enter the room and toe off my boots. With a hug for Ember, Scarlett climbs off the bed and leaves the room, closing the door behind her. I lose the rest of my clothes, climb into bed, and pull Ember's back against my chest, absorbing her heat. My body relaxes as our breaths sync, and I close my eyes. After several minutes the chaos residing inside me dissipates. Holding Ember is all I need. She's the air I need to breathe.

"Blake?"

"Yeah?"

"Don't let go."

I cling to her a little tighter. "Never."

20

EMBER

The tension in the clubhouse is so thick you can cut it with a knife, and the vibe reeks of retribution. Blake has yet to give me many details about what the club has planned, but I know enough about our way of life to know there is a threat of war.

Blake has been watching over me like a hawk. When he's not hovering around me, he's in Church or off with the guys. No matter how often I assure him I'm fine, he hasn't wanted to leave my side. Every time I walk into a room, eyes linger on my battered face.

I can tell he is harboring guilt for what happened to me, and I'm holding my own blame for allowing my sister to be put in a dangerous situation. What Scarlett went through won't go away with a good night's rest or be forgotten. My sister's trauma will stay with her forever, and that's on me. To ensure her safety, I need to send her away.

I recall my father's harsh words. Maybe he's right. As much as I love my sister, I'm no good for her.

"Mind if I join ya?"

Jake's request brings me out of my reverie, and I toss him a weak smile. "Sure." I pull the blanket tighter around my shoulders. I've sat outside for the past hour, alone with my thoughts, breathing the fresh air. Everyone could sense my mood and has been considerate enough to leave me alone. "As long as you don't ask me how I'm feeling," I muse, making Jake chuckle. There's a slight chill in the air as the sun begins to set behind the mountains, painting the sky in hues of pink and orange.

"Naw, I figure how you're feeling is a given." Jake hands me one of the two beers he is holding.

"Thanks." The two of us remain silent for a moment. I keep my eyes trained on the sunset while taking slow sips of my drink. I know why Jake is here. He's worried about me. "I'm okay," I say softly.

Jake takes a long pull from his beer. "No, you're not."

Leave it to Jake to call me out. He's never been a bullshitter or one to beat around the bush. Jake calls them like he sees them. I sigh. "No, I'm not."

I can feel Jake's intense stare drilling a hole in the side of my head. Turning, I face him. "It could have been my sister," I tell him softly, trying to hold back the tears.

"It wasn't," he counters.

"But—"

"Ember." Jake sets his beer down on the table in front of us. "You can't beat yourself up. Life is full of what-ifs. If you waste time on that kind of bullshit, then you're wastin' life."

I shut my eyes tight. "That's easier said than done, Jake."

"I know it is, darlin'. Let me ask you somethin'."

I open my eyes. "What."

"Had the shoe been on the other foot and Scarlett been in your position, would you want her beatin' herself up and blamin' herself for what happened?"

I scoff. "Of course not."

"You didn't put your sister in danger. You didn't knock her

unconscious and tie her up. You bear no responsibility for any of what happened. That's on the club."

I shake my head in protest. "Jake, no—"

He cuts me off by holding up his palm. "This is our burden to bear."

"I don't blame the club, Jake."

Jake's face softens. "I'm happy to hear that, sweetheart, but that doesn't change the fact that your safety is our responsibility, and we failed. For that, I'm sorry."

"You have nothing to be sorry for."

"Appreciate the sentiment, darlin', but we'll have to agree to disagree." He leaves no room for arguing.

I take another sip of beer and slump against the sofa. "I'm sending Scarlett away," I say with a sigh. Jake regards me but doesn't say anything. "I called her boyfriend and asked him to fly to Polson, and I'm going to ensure she gets on the plane when he leaves."

"Does Scarlett know?"

"No."

"You think that's what she will want?"

"Doesn't matter. It's what's best. I need my sister safe, and being here with me isn't safe. Not right now, at least." Before Jake can protest, I add, "I didn't make this decision because I don't believe the club can keep her safe; I did so because Scarlett doesn't belong here with me."

"Darlin'."

I toss my hand up. "It's what's best. Besides, Scarlett is happiest when she's with Keith. And she can still go to design school, just not here."

"You said her man is a mechanic. The club has plenty of work, and we can use another hand around the shop." When I don't respond, Jake continues. "The day I held a gun to a man's head and you got on the back of my bike was when you chose to take back your life. The girl I first met was so unsure of herself, and lost. Yet, you were brave enough to take a chance."

I can't hold back the tears.

"Over the years, I have enjoyed watching that lost girl turn into a beautiful, confident, successful woman. A woman I am damn proud of." Jake leans in closer. "The problem now is, you've lost some of that confidence, because you've let your piece of shit father get inside your head, making you think you're not good enough. You've let yourself believe you failed her. If you send your sister away, your father wins." Jake stands and kisses the top of my head. "The Ember I know wouldn't stand for that." Jake walks away, leaving me a crying mess with his words swarming around in my head. He's right. Jake is always right.

I haven't allowed my parents to control me for years, and I'm not about to start now.

"Fuck." Scarlett will kill me when Keith shows up. She has no idea. I went through her phone last night, found his number and called him, and insisted he fly to Polson. He's been beside himself and missing Scarlett like crazy for days and didn't hesitate at my invitation. He told me he'd be on the next flight out of North Carolina. Now I have to think of how to smooth things with Scarlett when Keith shows up. She's missing him like crazy, but hasn't wanted to make a choice between being with him or me. This brings me back to Jake's earlier statement. Why can't she have both? The only question is, will Keith be willing to uproot his life for Scarlett?

Knowing I need to talk to my sister, I toss the blanket aside, stand from the couch, and walk inside. I see Scarlett lounging in a chair across the room, laughing at something Bellamy said. When her gaze lands on me, her face brightens. "Hey."

"Hey." I make my approach. "What's up, kiddo?" I ruffle Bellamy's hair.

"Hey, Ember." She stands from where she was sitting on the

floor. "I'm going to find Lisa. She promised to show me how to make peanut butter cookies."

"Have fun." I watch her dash off searching for Lisa, then I turn back to Scarlett. "Can we talk?"

Her smile drops and is replaced with a look of worry. "Is everything okay?"

"Yes and no," I admit truthfully. "I did something that will possibly make you mad at me."

Scarlett's brow scrunches. "Mad at you?"

I nod. "I talked to Keith." The moment her boyfriend's name slips past my lips, her demeanor changes. "What! When? How did you get his number?"

"From your phone while you were sleeping."

Her lips thin into a firm line at my confession. "What did you and Keith talk about?"

"I asked him to come to Polson."

Scarlett's eyes widen. "Ember, please tell me you didn't."

"I'm sorry. I shouldn't have gone behind your back. It's just..."

"Just what, Ember?"

"I asked him to come here and take you back to North Carolina."

Scarlett shoots up out of her chair. "What?!"

"I thought it would be best if you left." I hesitate briefly, then add, "Because of what happened." My gaze automatically lingers on her bruised cheek.

My sister doesn't miss a beat. She brings her hand up to touch her bruised face and quickly drops it again. She doesn't immediately say anything; I know it's because she's studying me... putting the pieces together. "You're blaming yourself, aren't you?"

"I was," I admit. "Until someone made me realize I was wrong."

"I never blamed you, Ember."

I swallow past the lump in my throat. "I know. I...I was letting Dad get inside my head. I'm scared to death of something else happening to you. Knowing that you had to go through what you did, and that seeing what those men did to me might cause you to look at me differently; I couldn't bear it."

Scarlett's expression softens, and she wraps her arms around me. Our father's words cut me deeper than I let on, and now she knows. "I only want what is best for you."

"You are what's best for me." She leans back. "I just got you; I'm not letting you go that easily." We both start to cry.

"What about Keith?"

"What about him?"

"Come on, Scar. Don't lie. You're missing him like crazy."

She sighs. "I do. I miss him like you wouldn't believe. But how can I choose between my sister and the man I love? I want to be with both of you. If I stay, I'll miss him. If I go, I'll wish I was here with you."

"You don't have to choose." Scarlett and I both jump.

Standing just inside the clubhouse door is a stranger. He looks at least six feet tall, and his hair hangs to just above his shoulders, with just enough wave to give it a sexy, disheveled look. Standing beside him is Jake.

"Keith," Scarlett breathes and sprints across the room, straight into his arms. Keith buries his face in the crook of her neck. I suddenly stop regretting my decision to call him. Watching them, I see how he loves my baby sister and will do anything for her.

"I hopped on a plane as soon as I got your sister's call." He sets her back on her feet. Then he notices the bruise on her cheek, and even from across the room, I can see his body lock up.

"It's not as bad as it looks." Scarlett tries to ease Keith's worried reaction.

Keith's attention snaps to me, then to Jake.

Jake holds eye contact with my sister's boyfriend. "It's being dealt with," he assures him, his tone laced with venom. Keith, seeing something in Jake's expression, nods, satisfied with the silent promise Jake conveyed.

With his focus back on Scarlett, her mechanic cups her face and gently kisses her injured cheek. Sensing they need a few minutes of privacy, Jake and I make our way to the bar. Jake passes me a cold beer and grabs one for himself before sitting on the stool beside me. "When did Keith get here?" I ask.

"Showed up when we were out back," he tells me. "Austin was at the gate and let him in." He turns on the stool and leans his back against the bar. "I wanted to get a read on him."

"And?"

"Seems like a solid guy."

I smile. "Yeah. I like him for Scarlett."

Jake turns toward me. "I asked him what his intention was toward Scarlett."

I bite my lip, barely able to control my giggle. "What did he say?"

"Said he'd do whatever it took to make her happy. Then I asked if staying in Polson with her sister would make her happy."

I blink, stunned Jake had been so bold with a guy he just met. "What was his answer?"

A slow grin spreads across Jake's face. "The kid said he could fix cars anywhere."

21

BLAKE

It's been a madhouse around the clubhouse, and tension is high with the threat of retaliation lingering over our heads. My brothers and I have been on a continuous security rotation since this all started. At this level of lockdown, the men are the only ones allowed to leave the compound, and when we do, it's in pairs. As of this morning, Satan's Hounds have yet to be spotted outside their territory, since Demetri's men gave chase to the ones who got away following Ember and Scarlett's abduction.

The club's decision to let war come to us instead of taking the battle to the enemy is a first, but the choice to stay was an obvious one when my uncle sent men to fuck with us, hurting my woman while we met face-to-face with him and his men. It's safe to say they've been watching the club much closer than we realized. The coming war is about more than my uncle wanting Bellamy. He is out for blood—mine.

I stroll in from making another perimeter check and notice Bellamy sitting alone at the top of the stairs with her elbows propped on her knees and chin cradled in her hands. I climb the stairs and sit beside her. "Hey, kiddo."

"Hey." She sounds sullen and defeated.

"Are you okay?" I nudge her shoulder with mine.

"No."

"Want to talk about it?"

Bellamy sighs. "What's the point? It's not like anyone will tell me anything anyway." Bellamy remains silent momentarily before lifting her face and looking at me. "I've heard the whispering, and I know our uncle wants me back."

"He does." I admit to feeling like shit for not talking to her about it before now.

Bellamy's face falls, and she looks away. "Why?" Her voice is thick with fear.

My throat tightens. "They've deemed you the club's property for stealing money from them." I watch as the meaning of my words sinks in.

"All of this is my fault," Bellamy whispers, her voice quivering.

"Come here, kiddo," I open my arms and wait for my sister to turn around. She faces me, then leans in, and I embrace her. "You did what you needed to survive. Don't harbor guilt for anything that's happened."

"They won't ever stop, Blake. His torment will continue. I shouldn't be here."

"You are right where you belong, Bellamy. No matter what happens, I will protect you—the club will protect you. We are your family, and this is your home."

Later in the night, I lie awake in bed with Ember nestled into my side, her leg draped across my hip, her head resting against my shoulder, and her palm pressed against my chest. She's been sleeping peacefully for most of the night.

I gave up on sleep hours ago. We're counting down the clock after sending a massive *fuck you* to Satan's Hounds following killing another of their members. We didn't have to say anything. The moment the ones responsible for the assault on Ember and her sister returned one man short, I guarantee my uncle knew his man was maggot food.

The Kings have no intention of bending a knee to those cocksuckers. If the bastards want Bellamy bad enough to start a war, they'll have to bring the fight to us on our turf. Handing my sister over is not an option—it never was. Disgust settles in my gut. How does a mother offer her young daughter to a man, treating her life as disposable? Is she that far gone in her addiction that she is willing to toss her child to the wolves?

"Your heart is racing," Ember whispers. "Want to talk about it?"

"This shit with Satan's Hounds has me locked and loaded, anticipating anything happening at any moment. I'm in a constant state of fight mode." Ember rubs my chest, and I close my eyes, trying to focus on her soothing touch.

"She's only fifteen, Blake," Ember says, her voice full of sadness, and the weight of her statement feels like an elephant on my chest. "It's disgusting." She pauses, then adds, "But why all the destruction? I don't understand. Is Bellamy part of a bigger picture we don't know about?"

"I don't know, babe. I've wracked my brain asking myself the same thing, but the truth is, they are the type of men who feed off fear and destruction. They need no reason other than they want to." I take a deep breath and ponder whether I should continue discussing this with her, but she must understand who we're facing. "My uncle, the one running the club now, held a knife to my throat while my father put a bullet in my mom's head. These are the kind of men we're dealing with, babe. Pure evil. If the devil has soldiers walking among men, it's Satan's Hounds."

"Oh, Blake. I can't fathom living with a memory like that."

I let out a heavy breath and finally take the chance to share the rest of my story. "After my father and uncle killed the only family I had, they set the house on fire. Standing in the front yard, they made me watch as the place went up in flames, destroying as much evidence as possible, trying to ensure they left no trace of them ever being there." The emotions of that night come flooding back, and I feel them gathering in my eyes. "I stood there, frozen with fear and eaten up by an indescribably empty feeling, with tears and snot running down my face. I was physically outside the house, untouched by the fire, but my entire body felt as though it was inside, with my family, burning to ashes alongside them." Ember reaches over and takes hold of my hand. She remains quiet, but I can feel her love. My voice changes.

"'I don't want you. You have no one now. That's the price you are paying to stay alive. From this point on, I don't care what happens to you. You'd best forget I was here, boy. If trouble knocks at my door, I'll find ya' and kill ya'.' That's what my father said to me before he and my uncle left, leaving me alone." I fight like hell to hold my emotions at bay. I push through the pain and keep going, baring everything to Ember.

"Authorities didn't have any direction with the murders, and I wasn't talkin'. I had no next of kin, so I went into state custody— years of bouncing from one foster home to the next. I was rebellious, a troublemaker, and using drugs. Eventually, I was placed in a group home, which I ran away from at seventeen." I fall silent, collecting my thoughts, needing a moment to breathe.

Ember squeezes my hand. "Feel me, baby. I'm right here, and I'm not letting go." Her words cause what remains of the wall I had built around my heart to crumble.

"I was attempting to clean up my act, get off the drugs. I got a job just outside of my hometown workin' security at a strip club. It didn't pay much, but it was enough to pay for a cheap motel room and food daily. Anyway, one night, I stepped out for a smoke and to escape the noise for a few minutes. I caught a guy assaulting a woman when I walked out the back door." I flashback to the night.

"Hey!" I shout at the son of bitch who just slapped the shit out of the woman he has pressed against the brick wall. It's dark, so I can't distinguish his face from where I stand.

"Mind your motherfuckin' business, boy."

Great. Another drunk motherfucker is forcing himself on someone. "Get the fuck off her, asshole." I move in their direction and reach for my weapon.

"Fuck off before I..." His slurred words are cut short.

"Before you what?" I press the barrel end of the gun to his temple. He takes his hands off the woman. She gives me a look of thanks and then makes a quick escape. "I don't like sick fucks who get their kicks off assaulting women," I growl. The guy fully faces me, and my blood runs cold. It's been eight years since the last time I saw the man glaring back at me.

"You've messed with the wrong motherfucker." My father's face contorts with rage.

I realize he doesn't know who I am; not that he would. Every memory I have of him hits me all at once. All the raw rage I feel for his actions seeps from my pores. The need for vengeance is pulsing through my veins. "You once told me I was nothin' more than a waste of cum." My knuckles whiten as I grip the handle of the gun tighter. "You remember what I said that day?" I wait a beat for him to answer. His nostrils flare, and his eyes flash with recognition.

My father's face hardens, his expression turning hostile, then he smirks. "You ain't got the balls, boy." He sneers. "Should you pull the trigger, my men will hunt you down. And if you don't kill me, I will kill you. Either way, you're a dead man." His words are laced with venom, but I've been bitten by them too many times before, and they have no effect on me.

"A promise is a promise." I pull the trigger.

Ember pressing her lips against mine lifts the veil of my past, bringing me back to the present. She's propped on her elbow, looking down at me. "I took my father's life," I confess.

"Yes." She softly kisses me again.

"You don't think I'm a monster? Look at me. I'm the same as him: a cold-blooded killer." I look away, but Ember places her hand on my cheek and stops me.

"You are not your father, Blake. You are a good man who happens to be part of an MC, and who has sometimes killed to protect his family. You are nothing like your father, and you are not a monster." She presses her forehead against mine.

Silence hangs between us for several minutes while her words take root. My life with the Kings is not a reflection of my father. For him, killing was recreational—a blood sport. The Kings hold the club, loyalty, family, and love above themselves, which is why we kill and what we will die trying to protect.

The night I killed my father, I left California. I traveled as far as the money in my pocket allowed, and Polson, Montana, was where I ended up. For weeks I was paranoid, constantly looking over my shoulder, waiting to see one of my uncle's men. I needed to take off the edge and stop thinking about what I'd done and why I'd done it, so I reached for the one thing that would relieve me. I felt horrible for using it again, but not thinking about the past felt better. The problem was that I had no money. I set out to find a job to fix my cash and drug needs, and I landed a job at a lumber yard helping load and unload shipments. Although I had zero experience, the owner, Mr. Burton, was willing to give me a chance.

For weeks I kept my head down and worked hard. Life in Polson was good, but I was still using, and eventually, I lost my job. Mr. Burton told me he would put me back to work when I decided to get my life together and get clean. He was a nice older man. I had no ill feelings toward him, but that didn't stop me from blowing off steam over it. I took my ass to Charley's that night and drank—a lot. I ended up in a brawl with two men, both bigger than me. I didn't give a shit. I was wasted and feeling no pain.

They eventually left me slumped against the side of my beat-up car. I knew I was busted up damn good. It hurt like a motherfucker to breathe. At that moment, I didn't care. I felt myself passing out while I heard the rumble of motorcycles. Jake and the others found me that night. Doc looked after me and treated my injuries. The rest is history. Jake saw something in me I wasn't willing to see in myself. With support from strangers, I got clean and gained a job and a family in the process. My brothers knew everything about me, about my past. I hid nothing from them. Prospecting for the club wasn't easy, but I knew I wanted to be a part of something bigger than myself.

An eruption of gunfire shatters my reverie, and I scramble out of bed, racing to throw some pants on.

"Oh, my God!" Ember is in a panic fumbling to clothe herself. "The kids!" she cries out, stricken with fear.

I grab my gun. "Get to Bellamy and stay put." I storm out the door, running into the other men half-dressed and armed. We burst through the front door into the yard just in time to hear tires squealing and see the red lights of a retreating vehicle racing away from the compound gate. Just as fast as the chaos began, it appears to end. Jake barks orders for everyone to span out and secure the compound. My eyes land on Grey picking himself off the ground near the gate. I jog in his direction.

"Motherfuckers shot me," Grey growls, grinding his teeth, and I notice blood trickling in a thin stream down his forearm. "They threw something out the back of their vehicle, and whatever it was landed too far from the gate for me to make out what the hell it was."

I leave Grey and slip outside the gate, with my gun raised toward the road. It's dark as fuck; more so the farther I get from the dim light shining over the gated end of the driveway. I'm scanning my surroundings when the tip of my bare toe kicks against something solid. I turn my head from left to right, glancing in the direction of the road before squatting. On the ground is a body, but I still can't make out who. The sound of someone's approach has me standing and aiming my weapon.

"It's me, brother," Quinn says, holding his gun in one hand and a flashlight in the other.

"Got a body. Shine that light down here." I kneel again. The motionless body is lying on its side, so I roll them over. I'm unprepared for who it is, and I recoil with shock. His clothes are soaked in blood, and his face is nearly unrecognizable. On his chest is a crimson-stained piece of paper held in place by a knife; the blade plunged into his body.

"Jesus Christ, it's Charley," Quinn states, then faces toward the clubhouse and shouts *"Prez!"* His voice holds the heavy weight of urgency.

I keep my attention on Charley. His breathing is shallow, the rise of his chest barely noticeable. "He's breathing but barely."

I look over my shoulder to see Jake, Gabriel, and Logan barreling across the yard, heading toward us. All the blood drains from their faces when they arrive and take in Charley's condition and the bloody note stabbed to his chest.

TIME'S UP.

22

EMBER

The entire clubhouse is in complete chaos. The commotion and gunfire woke everyone.

"Keep the kids upstairs!" Logan shouts, sending a few women scrambling to keep the children from witnessing anything. So much blood is coming from the stab wounds in Charley's chest.

"He needs a hospital now," Emerson warns, her voice filled with urgency. "This is not something I can patch up here."

"Oh god, let him be okay," Lisa sobs as she watches Doc and Emerson fuss over Charley.

"Goddamit," Jake hisses. "Blake, Gabriel, help get him loaded. Logan, you ride out with us. I want you at my back. The rest of you stay behind."

With the orders doled out, the guys haul Charley off the floor, carry him out of the clubhouse, and place him in the back of the van. Everything happens fast. The next thing I know, Blake, Jake, Logan, and Gabriel peel through the compound gate. Bella walks up beside me, worry etched across her face.

23

BELLAMY

"I can't believe this is happening," I hear Bella say to Ember. They don't see me behind them, and before they notice I'm here, I turn on my heel and run up the stairs, brushing past Sofia.

"Bellamy, are you okay?"

I dodge the hand that reaches for me and ignore her question. Because I'm not okay. Nothing is okay and hasn't been since I showed up in Polson. Every terrible thing happening is my fault. First, Ember and her sister were kidnapped. Now that sweet old man Charley might die. There is only one way to stop Boner and my uncle Hellhound. I have to go back. I feel sick to my stomach at the thought of going back to California.

When I reach my room, I slam the door and lock it. I can't let anyone know what I'm about to do. I rush over to the bedside table to retrieve a notebook and pen. On a piece of paper, I write.

Blake, I'm sorry for everything. I shouldn't have come here. I didn't mean for all this to happen. I just wanted to be with my brother. I hope you don't regret meeting me because I could never regret meeting you. I love you, and I'm so happy you are my brother. I'm sorry Ember and Scarlett were hurt. Please tell everyone I'm sorry about their friend,

Charley. I hope he will be okay. I promise to make things better. I know what I have to do. Please don't be mad.

Love always, your sister.

Bellamy.

I rip the sheet from the notebook, fold it and place it on my pillow, then dig my book bag out from under the bed. I stuff a few articles of clothing inside, along with my medicine. Zipping the bag, I put it over my shoulders and then slip on my shoes. Walking over to the window, I shove it open. I poke my head out and look to make sure no one is around. Luckily my bedroom is on the back side of the compound, and the back deck that extends the length of the building is partially covered by roofing, which is right beneath the window. "You can do this. You have to do this." I psych myself up and slip out of the window, slowly sliding my body down the side of the house, not letting go of the window ledge until my toes touch a solid surface. I step softly to the edge of the metal roof and carefully lower myself to the ground. Tucking my body along the edge of the brick wall, I make my way toward the driveway of the clubhouse until the gate comes into view. I spot Grey on his phone, walking away from the entrance. I use the distraction to my advantage and make a run for it. The gate is closed, but I notice a gap between the bottom of the metal barrier and the ground. Dropping to my knees, I remove my bag and toss it over. Next, I lie flat on my belly and shimmy underneath the gate. Standing, I snatch my bag and run. It won't be long before someone notices I'm gone. I have no plan other than to distance myself from the clubhouse.

24

EMBER

I walk into the kitchen to find Lisa, Emerson, Lelani, Bella, and Alba sitting at the table. Grace, Sofia, Raine, and Mila are elsewhere, trying to calm the kids. Bella has the phone to her ear, a pained look on her face. "Okay," she whispers. "Let me know when you hear something." She hangs up.

"What did Logan say?" Mila asks.

"They just got to the hospital, and Charley is with the doctors now."

Sofia walks into the kitchen and heads to the refrigerator.

"Have any of you seen Bellamy?" I ask, my stomach still in knots from all the tension in the air.

"I thought she was with the other women helping care for the kids." Bella looks at me with concern.

I shake my head. "I just came from there."

"I ran into her upstairs just after they took Charley away, and she seemed pretty upset," Sofia tells me.

Relief washes over me. "I'm sure what happened with Charley has her shaken up. I'll go check on her."

"I hope she's okay," Bella says softly. "I'll come to find you when I hear more about Charley."

I give her a grateful smile and leave the kitchen.

As I go upstairs and down the hall, I pass Raine, who says, "Hey. Have you heard any news? I told Grace and Alba I would check."

"Unfortunately, no. Bella just talked to Logan, and Charley is with the doctors now. Logan said he'd call back with an update as soon as possible."

Raine closes her eyes and blows out a breath. "This is unbelievable."

"It's going to be okay." I pull Raine in for a hug. I realize I've had so much going on lately that I've neglected one of my best friends. Raine has been like a sister to me for the past few years. And recently, I haven't stopped to ask how she's been holding up with all that has happened. "Thank you for being a good friend, Raine. I haven't told you this, but I don't know what I would do without you. You've been great with Bellamy and with Scarlett."

Raine gives me a small smile. "I always got your back Ember."

"And I've always got yours," I tell her gently.

Leaving Raine to tell what little news we have on Charley to Grace and Alba, I continue my search for Bellamy. I knock when I reach her bedroom door. "Bellamy." When she doesn't answer, I try again. "Bellamy?" When she doesn't answer the second time, I try to open the door, but it's locked. "Bellamy!" I call out louder. "Come on and open the door."

"What's going on?"

I look over to see Austin striding toward me. "I don't know. She's not answering, and the door is locked," I tell him.

This time he tries knocking. "Bellamy, open up, sweetheart."

Austin and I look at each other. "Something's off, Austin."

"Stand back." He ushers me away from the door, raises his booted foot, and kicks the bedroom door open. The two of us storm in only to find the room empty. I check the bathroom, where I find dirty clothes on the floor. I look over at the bed to see her iPad lying there, along with her crumpled-up pajamas.

"See anything out of place?" Austin asks.

I shake my head. "No."

"Have you checked the basement?" Austin asks. "With all the commotion, she could have freaked out and found a hiding place. The girl has been through some shit."

He's right. "This whole thing is so fucked up."

"I'll go down there and look," he offers.

"Thanks."

After Austin walks out of the room, I turn to leave, but something out of the corner of my eye catches my attention: a folded sheet of paper lying on Bellamy's pillow. Walking over to the bed, I lift it off the pillow and open it up. As I scan the words, I feel dread in the pit of my stomach. "No." My eyes dart over to the window, which is open, a detail I skipped over before. Rushing over, I look out and inspect the yard, seeing no traces of Bellamy.

Wasting no time, I rear back, stick my leg through the window, and climb down. Once both feet touch the ground, I quickly spot imprints of shoes left behind on the soggy ground, thanks to the rain we had the night before. I follow them where they lead me. Once I clear the front of the clubhouse, the prints stop at the edge of the gravel drive that leads toward the entrance gate. Bellamy hasn't been missing for long, so she couldn't have gotten far. I hesitate for a split second, thinking I should go back and find Austin, but against my better judgment, I go ahead without him. Sprinting across the yard, I make it to my car. *Shit*. I panic. I left my keys inside. Then I remember the spare key hidden beneath my seat in a little black key box. I fish it out and start the car. With shaky hands, I pull my phone out and type in the code for the gate. Seconds later, the gate opens. I shift the car into gear and step on the gas, my tires spinning, kicking up dust and rocks. Once I've cleared the gate, I head toward town.

All sorts of horrible thoughts start running through my mind about the bad things that can happen to a young girl walking alone at night on a dark road. Not to mention the other club is out here somewhere, determined to wreak havoc on anyone associated with the club.

My cell starts to ring, the screen lighting up with Austin's name. I'm about to answer it when I spot a figure up ahead, walking along the side of the road. *Bellamy.* I breathe a sigh of relief. My cell stops ringing, then starts up again. This time it's Bella's name that pops up. I ignore it for the time being. My sole focus is Bellamy. Hearing my approach, she peers over her shoulder, then she freezes. She throws her arm up to cover her eyes to block out the glare of my headlights. "Bellamy!" I shout out my open window. I pull off to the side of the road and jump out of the car. "Thank God I found you." I rush up and take her into my arms.

She starts to sob. "I'm sorry, Ember. It's all my fault. Everything is my fault."

"Shh," I console her. "Nothing is your fault. You didn't have to run away like this, Bellamy. Nobody blames you for anything."

"But it's true." Her body shakes violently. "You were hurt because of me, and now that old man might die. All because I'm here."

"Look at me." I grip her shoulders to make sure I have her full attention. "What happened to me and what happened to Charley is not your fault. Not one person blames you. I have never seen your brother so happy. Blake didn't think he had any family left, then you showed up. You have given Blake something nobody else can, and that's special. Your brother loves you, Bellamy. We all do."

Bellamy sniffles. "I wanted to make things right. I thought if I left and went back, you all would be safe."

"Sweetheart, you are not going back to those people. The Kings are your family now. You're stuck with us forever." I wipe a stray tear from Bellamy's cheek as she cracks a watery smile. "What do you say we go home? Everyone is worried sick about you."

"I'd like that."

Bellamy and I are walking to my car when we startle at the thunderous sound of a large engine and blinding headlights barreling toward us. At the last second, the large truck swerves, looking to strike us where we stand. With lightning-quick reflexes, I grab hold of Bellamy and dive out of the way, seconds before the truck slams into the back end of my car. I land on top of her in the ditch and cover her head as crunching metal crashes around us.

Through a daze, I stand, pulling Bellamy with me. My eyes widen with shock, and the adrenalin floods my veins, making my heart feel like it will beat out of my chest. Blake's sister clings to me, fear written all over her face as we take in my mangled car.

25

BLAKE

"Goddammit!" Jake rages, putting his fist through the van's window, sending broken glass flying everywhere. He pulls his hand back, his knuckles cut and bleeding. "Those motherfuckers got the drop on us, and now Charley's knockin' on death's door because of it."

I look back at the hospital, and guilt eats at my insides. Charley is a good man. He doesn't deserve to be in there lying on an operating table fighting for his life right now. I look down at my blood-stained hands. There's only one way to make this right. My phone rings, jerking me from my thoughts, and I answer, not bothering to see who the call is from. "Yeah?"

"Blake." Austin's voice filters into my ear, and the tone of his voice causes the muscles in my body to lock up. "Ember and Bellamy are missing."

My heart hammers and panic surges through me. "How long?"

"Last time I had eyes on Ember was thirty minutes ago when she was looking for your sister," Austin informs me, then yells, "Fuck!"

Jake locks eyes with me. "Tell him and the others to stay put. If

195

another person leaves the compound, I'll have their asses." I relay the message, then disconnect the call.

This cannot be happening.

"Head back toward the clubhouse. There's only one way to town from there, and if she travels it, we'll find her." Jake fires up his bike and takes off with Logan falling in behind him. I jump into the van as Gabriel starts the engine, and we take off after them.

I punch the dashboard repeatedly as my emotions reach their boiling point. "Fuck!" My body shakes at the level of rage spreading through me, fueled by my terror. "She fucking knows better." I curse that Ember left the safety of the clubhouse, then grow angrier because Bellamy left too. I think back to the conversation I had with Bellamy this morning, and though she fears what's happening between the clubs, she's harboring a massive amount of guilt, thinking and trying to shoulder the blame. It finally dawns on me that Bellamy must have left for those reasons, and my heart sinks to my stomach, knowing she is willing to sacrifice herself for all of us. "Shit!" I hit the dashboard one more time once I piece it all together. "She left to give herself to Satan's Hounds, and Ember went looking for her."

Through my outburst and revelation, Gabriel remains quiet as we speed down the road, keeping pace with Prez and Logan, who are a couple of car lengths ahead of us. The silence encapsulating the inside of the van leaves me with a rabbit hole of maddening thoughts, conjuring up the worst-case scenario—finding Ember and my sister... dead.

In the distance, just beyond the bridge, we notice a warm, illuminating light and billowing gray-white smoke pluming upwards. On the other side of the bridge, an overturned vehicle is engulfed in flames. "It's Ember's car!" I leap from the van before Gabriel brings it to a complete stop and I race toward the inferno. "Ember! Bellamy!" I get as close as the scorching heat will allow, trying to see inside. I try getting closer, ignoring the stinging heat on my skin. "Ember!" I shout her name with so much intensity that my lungs burn. I nearly lose my footing when Logan pulls me back from the flames. I jerk from his hold and pull at my hair while staring at Ember's vehicle. The smell of burning plastic fills the air, penetrating my lungs and stinging my eyes. All I hear is the roaring of the fire, my heartbeat whooshing in my ears, and the voice inside my head. *They are not dead. They are not dead.*

I feel myself unraveling.

Dread, fear, and guilt claw at my throat.

I can't breathe.

"Blake." I hear the baritone of Jake's voice, but it sounds far away. "Blake, goddammit, snap out of it!" This time, I turn away from the flames to see Jake standing before me. "Ember and Bellamy are not in the car." He makes the statement with certainty that should put me at ease, but the alarm in his eyes installs a new sense of urgency in me. "Satan's Hounds have them."

My body goes numb. "Where?"

"Charley's."

I don't have time to question or think about my actions. Later, if I'm still alive, I'll happily accept repercussions for taking another brother's bike and going rogue, half-cocked, without consulting Jake. I sprint across the street, hop on Logan's bike, and take off, heading for Charley's bar. Though my mother believed in a higher power, I've never been much of a religious man. But I'm praying now and hoping like hell the Almighty is listening. *Keep my woman and my sister safe. Don't let anything happen to them. I don't give a damn what happens to me. I'm begging you, please protect my family.*

A short time later, I'm rolling into the bar's parking lot, which is littered with probably a dozen unmanned bikes. I approach the entrance and arm myself as I dismount Logan's ride. At the same time, a short bald motherfucker walks out of the door with his gun aimed in my direction, and I shoot the bastard before he gets the chance to pull his trigger. The biker falls to the ground, his body propping the door open. I hear tires squealing and loose gravel spraying everywhere, peppering the parked motorcycles as Jake flies into the parking lot. Close behind are Gabriel and Logan in the van. I step over the dead Satan's Hound and enter the bar before my brothers can stop me.

Nine Hounds meet me, a few of whom now have guns aimed at my face. I keep my gun raised in front of me, scanning the bar until my eyes land on my uncle, Hellhound, kicked back in a chair with his feet propped on the table at the far side of the room.

"Blake." He pauses to take a shot of whiskey, then slams the glass against the table, laughing. "You've got balls; I'll give you that. Reminds me of your father."

His words further fuel the rage swirling inside me. "I am nothing like my father," I seethe.

My uncle looks past me. "And here I thought we would be hosting seven Kings instead of one." He jerks his chin. "Toad, Boner, Tater, and Dutch, get your asses outside. You see someone, shoot 'em."

Just as his men rush out the entrance, gunfire breaks out. I remain rooted in a standoff with the remaining Satan's Hounds, keeping my gun aimed at my uncle throughout the ongoing gun battle outside the bar.

There's a moment of dead silence after the gunfire ceases before Jake, Logan, and Gabriel appear. "I hope you don't mind us evening out the playing field." Jake moves forward, flanking my side while Logan and Gabriel keep our backs covered.

My uncle's face contorts with anger. He pours another shot. "I see you received my message. I got to give the old man credit. He put up a good fight. I must admit I've enjoyed this little cat-and-mouse game." He downs the liquor. "But I'm bored." Hellhound snaps his fingers, and one of the remaining five men strolls into the restroom, returning with Ember and Bellamy, their hands bound in front of them.

"Blake!" Bellamy cries, and the fear I see in her eyes is gut-wrenching. My uncle reaches out, snagging Ember by the arm, and pulls her onto his lap. She fights against his hold, but another Satan's Hounds member takes his aim from me and points it at Ember, making her comply. My eyes connect with hers. "She's a sweet piece of ass." I feel my uncle eyeing me as he touches Ember, but my focus is on my woman and the single tear rolling down her cheek. It's taking all my self-control to keep from pulling the trigger, but I won't chance it with Ember in the way.

"Get your filthy fucking hands off my woman," I growl, my jaw clenched with hostility.

"Or what?" Hellhound retorts. "You'll kill me?" He chuckles. "I'm holding all the cards here." He tosses Ember to the side. My uncle takes a swig straight from the whiskey bottle, then wipes his mouth with the back of his hand. "My game, my rules."

One of my uncle's men, standing off to my left, makes a sudden move. "Take another step, and I'll kill you, motherfucker," Logan warns the biker, but the dumb fuck must have the attention span of a flea. I watch him take another step while reaching beneath his cut. That's when I hear Logan fire his weapon, sending the piece of shit flying backward, crashing into a nearby table and chairs.

The room becomes a conduit for electricity as yet another Hound takes his last breaths, but before anyone else can make another move, a distant rumble slices through the silence in the room. From the corner of my eye, I see Jake smirk. "That would be the rest of my men." My uncle's nostrils flare, and he cranes his neck. Jake continues, "You made a grave mistake bringing your club into Kings territory. You may have got the drop on us tonight, but we are prepared for war. You won't be going home tonight. Not unless it's in a body bag." Jake's words drip with venom.

My uncle stands, sending the chair he sat in flying backward, then reaches out, jerking Ember in front of him, using her as a human shield. Bellamy tries pulling free of her captor, but he tightens his hold on my sister.

My uncle releases a manic laugh. "I'm not goin' down just yet, motherfuckers."

I feel like someone has a stranglehold around my neck, and I'm choking on my breath. My eyes dart between Ember and Bellamy, trying to work out how to get them out of this alive.

Simultaneously, the sound of a rifle penetrates the air, and the son of a bitch holding Bellamy slumps to the floor.

"Bellamy, run!" Ember screams, and my sister dashes back toward the door leading to the kitchen. Another of my uncle's men reacts, charging after her, and Jake shoots the cocksucker in the head.

There are two Satan's Hounds men left, standing between us and their President. I still have my gun aimed at my uncle, whose face is twisted and red with anger. "Either I'm walkin' out of here alive, or she's dead," he spews.

Going into this battle, I never questioned what I would do to keep my family safe. I quickly toss my gun to the floor and show my hands. "I'll take her place." I offer my life for Ember's, and tears stream down her face.

My uncle stares at me, shaking his head. "You value this whore's life more than yours, which means I can walk out of here through the front door." While he's talking, I feel someone slip a hand beneath my cut, placing what feels like a blade between my back and the waistband of my jeans. "So why the fuck would I trade that for a worthless piece of shit like you?"

"Because you'd be trading her life for the man who killed your brother," I confess and watch his face contort with rage. "My woman walks, and I leave with you."

My uncle contemplates my offer. "You leave here with me, and your men stand down. If you agree to that, then I'll hand over the bitch."

I look at Jake. He nods, though his eyes convey the unspoken. Faced with the same scenario, he would do the same—all my brothers would. I look back at my uncle. "Done."

I approach my uncle with raised hands and close the distance while Ember stares at me with red-rimmed eyes. "Blake," she whispers. Thinking I will never hear my name pass her lips again feels like a bullet to the chest. Once I'm in arm's reach, my uncle shoves Ember forward and takes hold of me instead.

Ember looks back at me.

"It's okay," I tell her, keeping my emotions subdued and tone even. "Go."

She stares at me a minute longer, then moves across the room. Logan, Jake, and Gabriel keep their guns aimed at the Satan's Hounds, ensuring Ember safely exits the bar.

My uncle fists my cut, spins us, and pins my back against the wall. Over his shoulder, I take in my brothers keeping watch. There's a good chance I will die tonight, but I'll leave this life knowing what family means and what love feels like. "Want to know a little secret?" My uncle shoves me and keeps his voice to a harsh whisper while holding his gun under my chin. "I knew you killed my brother. The bitch you valiantly saved that night saw you do it." His eyes darken. "Too bad she had to die too." He brings his face inches from mine, baring his teeth. I slowly reach behind my back, wrap my hand around the knife's handle, and slip it down to my side as he continues, "I've been lookin' for you, Blake. For a long time. I had other plans once I learned of your whereabouts. I was going to destroy everyone and everything around you, making you suffer like we did all those years ago. Your sister's mother should have never run her mouth about you. She almost fucked up my entire plan."

"Looks like she succeeded. Your men are dead while my club and those I care for are still breathin'. You have nothing." I grip the blade's handle tighter.

My uncle smirks. "I have you. You're mine. In the end, I always get what I want. I win."

A couple of seconds tick by before I make my move. If I die, I'll go out fighting. My brothers notice what I'm attempting. They shoot the remaining Satan's Hounds simultaneously as I thrust the knife into Hellhound's side, stabbing him twice in rapid succession. With my other hand, I grab his gun, place my finger between his and the trigger and look him in the eyes. "You lose, motherfucker." I plunge the blade into the side of his neck and rip it out. His hands fly to his neck, desperate to control the blood pouring from his body. Within a second, he's on the floor in a pool of blood, gasping his last breaths.

I retrieve my gun off the floor, and before passing my brothers, I look at them. "I know I fucked a few things up tonight, but thanks for havin' my back."

Jake grips my shoulders. "We're family." He jerks his chin. "Take them home."

I walk out the front door into the parking lot, where Austin, Reid, Grey, Sam, and Quinn are waiting, and on the ground lie the other dead Satan's Hounds. "Blake." Ember rushes at me. She grabs my face, kissing me, and I wrap my arms around her waist and hold her tight. I notice my sister stepping out of the van. She makes a beeline across the parking lot and joins the huddle, crying and sniffling.

"Hey, kiddo." I get her attention, and she lifts her head and looks at me. Her nose is red, and her cheeks are flushed. "Everything is going to be okay." She nods, then buries her face against my ribcage again.

"Is he dead?" Bellamy asks, her voice muffled.

"Yes." I keep my reply simple but think about her mom. She deserves to know and rip that Band-Aid off now. "Bellamy, look at me." I wait for her to lift her face. "Your mom is..." Fuck, it's hard for me to say.

Bellamy's lip wobbles. "Is she dead?"

"Yeah, kiddo." I kiss the top of her head. "I'm sorry."

Bellamy cries harder, clutching at me. Regardless of their past, she loved her mom. I lift my sister in my arms and look at Ember. "Let's go home."

It's been several hours since Ember, Bellamy, and I arrived at the clubhouse. The rest of the members are finally back after taking care of the aftermath between us and my uncle's club. Nikolai and a few of his father's men, who watched the families while the club took care of business, left a few minutes ago. Charley made it through surgery and is in intensive care, where he will likely stay for several days before being moved to a regular room to finish the recovery process. He lost a fuck ton of blood and sustained a couple of broken ribs, a concussion, and liver damage from one of the stab wounds. The knife in his chest barely missed his heart. If the blade had been longer, Charley wouldn't be here. He's lucky to be alive.

For now, the clubhouse is quiet.

With Bellamy finally asleep, Ember and I head to her room. "She's devastated." Ember falls to the bed. "I wish I could make the pain go away." She removes her shoes.

I can still smell the whiskey stench on my uncle's breath, so I kick off my boots and shed my clothes.

"We'll see her through it, babe." I stroll across the room and grab my woman by the hand, pulling her off the bed and leading her to the bathroom. I reach behind the shower curtain, turn on the water, and then face her. She moves to remove her shirt, but I stop her. "Let me do it."

Ember gives me a soft smile. "I should be taking care of you."

I lift the shirt over her head. "I need this, babe." I move to her jeans and push the denim down her hips and thighs, removing her panties. Ember steps out of her clothes, kicking the garments to the side. She steps into the shower, and I join her. Together we stand beneath the water, soaking in the heat. I take her favorite lavender-scented shampoo from the shelf, squeeze some into the palm of my hand and massage it through her hair into a thick lather. Ember closes her eyes, letting out a soft moan. My cock responds to her naked body and the sounds she makes. I ignore the aching need to fill her pussy full of my cock. This isn't about sex. I'm taking care of my woman. Once the soap is rinsed from her hair, I repeat the process with conditioner before applying body wash to a loofah and washing every inch of her body. Doing the same for me, Ember washes my hair and lathers my body. We take care of each other.

Once the water runs cold, I dry her off and brush her hair before tending to myself, then get her settled into bed.

I slide in behind her, pulling her body against mine, and melt into the warmth of our bodies. I've got a real chance at happiness without constantly looking over my shoulder now, and I'm not about to waste it. I want a life with Ember, and that starts with us building a solid foundation to stand on. It's a new day and a fresh start.

I nuzzle my face in the crook of her neck. "You ready for this? You and me?"

"I've been ready for two damn years."

"I'm sorry it took me so long to get here." I close my eyes and sink into the peace I only get from holding her.

"You'll make up for it." I hear the smile in her tone.

I shift, roll Ember to her back, and hover over her. I pause before kissing her. "Damn right, I will."

EPILOGUE

"Will you sit down already? You're making me dizzy." I close the laptop and set it on the sofa beside me. I've been trying to work on my next book project, but no matter what room I retreat to, Blake finds me. And all he does is pace and look at his watch every five minutes. I'd find him adorable for being brotherly over his sister's first day of school if I weren't so annoyed.

Standing, I walk over to Blake and wrap my arms around his waist. "She'll be here any minute. She's riding home with Remi and her friends, and they probably stopped by to see Grace at the bakery for a snack. You have got to chill a little."

"I'm being chill," Blake grunts.

"Mmhmm," I tease, rolling my eyes.

"It's a big day for her," he says, his tone full of worry.

My expression softens. "I know it is."

Bellamy told us she hated school because kids bullied her and called her nasty names just because of who she was associated with. Blake and I assured her things would be different here in Polson. Even Remi explained to her that none of the kids would mess with anyone linked to the club. Since Bellamy and Remi have become close, she introduced Bellamy to her small circle of friends over the summer. By the time the first day of school rolled around, Blake's sister was excited to attend school for the first time.

Reaching up on my tiptoes, I press my lips to his. "You're an amazing big brother, you know that?"

"Thanks, baby."

Suddenly, the clubhouse door bursts open, and Bellamy practically skips through, wearing the biggest smile with Remi trailing behind her.

"Hey!" I greet them. "How was your day?"

Bellamy tosses her book bag on the sofa. "The best!"

Blake visibly relaxes, and I toss him an *I told you so* look. "Well, I want to hear all about it." I plop down on the sofa beside her.

"Yeah, Bellamy," Remi sing songs. "Tell them about Preston."

Blake jumps in. "Who the fuck is Preston?"

"A boy from school," Bellamy tells her brother.

"Oh my god!" I squeal. "You met a boy?" I ignore Blake and the tiny vein in his forehead that looks like it's about to burst.

"Not just any boy," Remi chimes in. "Preston is Captain of the football team. Every girl at school wants to be with him, but he asked Bellamy to sit with him at lunch."

"Really?" I say with a breathy sigh.

"Wait a fuckin' minute." Blake tries to cut in again but fails to be acknowledged.

Bellamy blushes. "He's so cute, Ember. And he was so sweet. After lunch, he met me outside all my classes so he could carry my backpack."

"Did you all hear me?" Blake grumbles. "I don't want any fuckwad carryin' my sister's book bag or sittin' with her at lunch."

"Come on, you guys." I grab Bellamy's hand. "Let's get some ice cream, and you can finish telling me about Preston."

"Okay!" Bellamy and Remi say in unison. The three of us skip to the kitchen, leaving a disgruntled big brother behind.

"Hey! I'm not done talkin' about this!"

The next day, the entire family is at the clubhouse, celebrating the opening of Alba and Leah's bookstore, which was a huge success. True to my word, I made my first public debut as Ellise Brooks. I was a bundle of nerves leading up to the event and didn't think anyone would show up to meet me, but by the time the store opened, a line of people wrapped around the block. I signed so many books today that I thought my fingers would fall off. The local community center knitting club, which consists of about a dozen elderly women, also has its own little book club. And their latest book series they were reading and discussing was none-other than yours truly. Who would have thought? Then we had our long-time Polson residents, who were shocked to find out they had a real-life romance author living in their town. I'll admit it felt good being gushed over.

A pair of arms wrap around me from behind, bringing me out of my wandering thoughts, and I breathe in Blake's familiar scent. "What ya thinkin' about, baby?"

My body melts against his as I take in our family milling around the yard and the kids playing in the pool. "I was thinking about how perfect today has been."

Blake kisses the spot below my ear. "I'm proud of you, Vita Mia."

Tipping my head back, I peer up at Blake through my lashes. "Why do you call me Vita Mia?"

"My mother used to call me Vita Mia. It means *my life.*"

"Blake," I say with a hushed breath.

"You are my life, Ember. Always."

"I love you," I tell him.

"I love you too, baby."

It's late afternoon and I'm sitting on the edge of the new swimming pool Jake had installed last summer. The children spent months relentlessly begging him for one and in true Jake fashion when it comes to the kids, he caved. I'm watching Bellamy play Marco Polo with Breanna and Jake, Logan and Bella's two kids, when the sound of two men arguing across the yard catches my attention.

"Your ribs can kiss my ribs' ass." Quinn takes a stance against Reid.

"You wish, motherfucker. Nobody wants that dried-up shit you call barbeque," Reid counters.

Quinn points his tongs at Reid. "Take that back."

Reid crosses his arms over his chest. "I'm not takin' shit back."

"What are they fighting about?" Bellamy asks, making me giggle.

I turn to my right, where Gabriel and Blake are standing. "Es estúpido." Gabriel shakes his head.

Blake glances at me and smirks.

I turn back to Bellamy. "It's tradition."

She gives me a bewildered look. "Tradition?"

"Yeah." Blake jerks his chin toward the two men arguing about barbeque. "Every year, Reid and Quinn try to outdo each other on the grill, and each year they make us pick a winner."

"Whose turn is it to win this year?" I ask him.

He grins. "Reid."

"Wait." Bellamy holds up a hand. "How do you know who the winner is if you haven't tasted the food yet?"

"We alternate who wins each summer. This time it's Reid, and next summer will be Quinn's turn." Blake shrugs. "Keeps the score even."

Bellamy laughs. "Do they know you all pick the winner in that order?"

"No fuckin' clue," he chuckles.

She giggles and paddles back over to play with the little kids. Holding out a hand, Blake pulls me to my feet. He runs his finger along my bikini strap, then over the top of my nipple, causing my skin to prickle. "Like your bathing suit, babe."

My swimsuit is a simple two-piece lavender number I found while shopping with Bellamy and Scarlett the other day. Bellamy found it and said it reminded her of my hair. "Thanks," I say in a hushed voice. Blake's pupils dilate, and his nostrils flare as he takes in my erect nipples. I tug on his belt loops, pulling him flush against my body. A gasp escapes my lips when I feel his erection against my stomach. We search each other's eyes, and I know he's thinking the same thing as me. "Let's go." Blake grabs my hand, and I run to keep up with his long strides as he leads us inside.

"Hey, brother," Sam tries to say to Blake, only to be cut off when Blake barks out "later" without breaking stride. Behind us, I can hear several women's soft laughter. When we reach my bedroom, Blake kicks the door shut, and I have no time to react before he's on me. "Bikini off, on the bed, and spread your legs wide for me," Blake orders.

Not wanting to deny my man anything, I strip out of my bikini and sit on the edge of the bed. His gaze stays laser-focused on me as I slowly spread my legs.

"Stay just like that. I want your pussy dripping wet for me." Blake removes his cut and hangs it on the hook beside the door. Next, he toes off his boots while reaching behind his head and pulling his shirt off. His abs ripple with each movement as he unbuckles his belt and tugs down his jeans. I watch with hooded eyes as his large cock springs free. I hum in anticipation, pussy clenching at the thought of having his cock inside me.

"This is going to be hard and fast." Blake climbs onto the bed and covers my body with his. He takes my mouth with his, his tongue teasing the seam of my lips. When I open for him above and below simultaneously, he thrusts inside me, and I tear my mouth away from his. *"Blake,"* I cry out.

"Fuck," he says with a raspy growl. "This pussy was made for me."

"Yes," I hiss, meeting him thrust for thrust.

"I need you to get there, baby. Rub your clit for me."

I slip my hand between our bodies until I find my clit. "I'm close." As soon as the words fall off my tongue, my orgasm crashes through me. I throw my head back as white flashes of lights dance behind my eyelids. Blake palms my hip in a bruising grip as he rides out his orgasm. Burying his face in the crook of my neck, he floods my pussy with his release, leaving us both gasping for breath.

"I like hard and fast," I pant.

A few minutes later, I walk out of the bathroom after cleaning up to find Blake fully dressed and slipping his cut back on. "Get dressed. I want to show you something."

Fifteen minutes, I'm on the back of Blake's bike, and we're riding away from the compound. It takes a little while before he pulls onto a familiar road leading to his workshop. My eyes go big when I'm met with a fully-built house frame, and at least a dozen men in hard hats busy at work. We stop, and Blake kicks the kickstand down and cuts the engine. I climb off the bike and whip off my helmet. "You're building a house?" My stomach drops at the thought of not having him around at the clubhouse twenty-four-seven. But in hindsight, I can see why he'd move out now that he has Bellamy.

"Yes," he answers.

I swallow past the lump in my throat and plaster on a smile. "I'm so happy for you. A house will be good for you and Bellamy." I quickly look away, so Blake doesn't see the sadness I desperately try to conceal.

"Baby." Blake grabs my arm and forces me to meet his gaze. "The house is for all of us," he says.

"What?"

"I want this place to be our home. You, Bellamy, and me."

"You...you want me to live here with you?"

"Where I go, you go, Vita Mia." Blake cups my face in the palms of his hands. "So, what do ya say, baby? You want to go on this crazy ride with me?"

I blink up at Blake with a watery smile. "Yes." Then he kisses me hard and deep.

For the next hour, Blake and a contractor hired by Kings Construction show us around the site, going over the floor plans. He asks my opinion on every detail, making sure I'm happy with his original vision of what he wants our future home to look like. By the time the tour is over, I've already envisioned how each room will be decorated, which Blake said was up to me. His exact words were, "I don't give a shit about wall color and furniture. As long as I have a big bed to fuck you in, I don't care what you do with the rest."

Straddling his bike, Blake lights a cigarette and hands me my helmet. "You up for one more ride?"

I take the helmet from him and grin. "Absolutely."

When Blake asked me to ride with him, I wasn't expecting him to take me on a five-day trip to Georgia. Not that I was complaining. We stopped and saw many sights along the way, and Blake had booked some fantastic bed and breakfasts to crash in. Our trip served two purposes. First, Blake wanted some alone time with me. He said with all the chaos surrounding the club over the past few months, we haven't had a chance to be a couple without all the drama. He wanted to concentrate on being together without interruptions, which was sweet. The second reason was why I gave him the silent treatment on our third day on the road. I'll admit now my attitude toward him was childish. Blake rode out my antics, and in the end, I saw he was right. That led us here, to me standing on my parents' doorstep. I haven't set foot on this property in so long that it feels almost foreign. My family has lived in the same gated community since I was a little girl.

When we approached the gate, Blake pulled his phone out and texted Reid, who quickly helped him override the system. He also tapped into my parents' security system along with the neighbors, so there will be no trace we were ever here.

Now, Blake is hanging back by his bike in the driveway per my request. I need to do it on my own. Taking a deep breath, I lift my hand and ring the doorbell. My mouth is dry, and my stomach is in knots. But knowing the man I love is here gives me the courage to say what I came here to say. To get the closure I deserve.

A moment later, the door opens, and I come face-to-face with my mother. Dressed in her signature pantsuit and a string of pearls, she looks as she always has. The pleasant smile she has on her face drops when recognition sets in. "What are you doing here?" Her eyes rake over me. My mother takes in my tight jeans, motorcycle boots, and Harley tee. Her face twists in disgust when she sees the ink on my arms and the vibrant color of my hair. "I suggest you leave before your father sees you."

"I'm not going anywhere until I say what I've come here to say." I stand my ground.

"Who's at the door, dear?" My dad comes up behind my mother, placing a hand on her shoulder. His body goes rigid when he sees me standing here. "What the hell is the meaning of this? You have some nerve showing up at our house," he sneers.

I lose some nerve until my father's eyes flick over my shoulder, and I feel Blake's looming presence nearby. My dad visibly swallows, no doubt remembering his last encounter with Blake.

"Like I told Mom, I came here to say something to you two. Once I've said my piece, I'll go, and you'll never see me again."

My father lifts his nose in the air. "I don't have time for whatever this is."

"You'll make time," comes the rumbly voice behind me.

My father purses his lips but stays quiet.

"What I wanted to say is *I forgive you*." At my words, my mother jerks as though she's been slapped, but I continue. "I forgive you for being shitty parents. I forgive you for putting insane expectations on me at such a young age. I forgive you for caring more about what others thought than your daughters' feelings and well-being. I even forgive you for believing whatever bullshit story that asshole Devan made up when he took me on that trip to Vegas. The one where I called you and asked for help. The one where I tried to explain that he gambled away all his money and mine, and when he couldn't pay up, he offered me up on a silver platter instead. He left me in that bar with a bunch of criminals who had in mind to do god knows what with me."

I pause to catch my breath. "Instead, I want to thank you. Because of you, I could find my true family, who took me and gave me a safe haven, no questions asked. I know what you see when you look at me. The beauty of that is I don't give two fucks what you or anyone else thinks. Something you know nothing about." I peer over my shoulder at Blake, who is grinning with pride. "I have the kind of family who will have my back no matter how often I screw up. They are the kind of family who will walk through hell and back for the people they love." I turn back to my parents. "I have the kind of family who supports all my hopes and dreams.

They will stand beside me through the good and the bad. Another thing you know nothing about." When I finish my speech, my father is ready to spit nails. As for my mother, she almost looks ashamed. Without another word, I turn on my heel and walk away from the past that's been suffocating me in silence, and I walk toward my future.

"We have one last stop, babe!" Blake yells over the rumble of the bike's motor. We head toward another location a few miles from my parents. This neighborhood is not gated, but it is just as pretentious. The motorcycle stands out like a sore thumb as we ride down several streets until he stops us in front of a large two-story home nestled into a cul-de-sac. I take in the picture-perfect landscape and imagine everything inside is decorated in various shades of beige. When my eyes land on the shiny brand-new black BMW sitting in the driveway, my gaze shifts to the tag that reads DEVAN#1.

"Fuckin' pussy," Blake quips.

"Is this...?" I clutch Blake's shoulders as a gamut of emotions slither through me, one of them being rage.

Blake leans down and unstraps the baseball bat he has rigged to the side of the bike. I noticed it there this morning but didn't question him about what it was for. "Payback's a bitch, and it's time this motherfucker antes up." Blake passes me the bat. I take it from him with blood rushing to my ears. God, I love this man. "Do your worst, baby."

Bat in hand, I walk up the driveway toward the shiny car. The whole trek up the driveway, that stupid plate mocks me. A scream tears through my throat as I strike the back end. The plate clatters to the concrete below. Next, I slam the bat into each one of the taillights. Tiny shards of red debris fly around my face. On a roll, I take out the left back passenger window before moving on to the driver's side. Adrenaline courses through my veins. I'm having an out-of-body experience with my rage. Time seems to slow as I shatter every window on Devan's precious car. I don't give a shit that it's not the same car he traded me for. It's what it represents. I repeatedly bring the bat down on the hood, doors, and trunk. I take out the side mirrors and the headlights. I'm knocked out of my terroristic euphoria when a man comes running out of the house in boxers and a t-shirt. Devan. Aside from the extra twenty pounds he's carrying around his midsection, he looks the same, and I can see the start of a receding hairline from where I'm standing.

"My car! What are you doing to my car!" he bellows. "I'm calling the police..." The threat dies on his tongue when he sees who's responsible for the damage to his vehicle. Devan's mouth falls open as recognition sets in. "Ember?"

I stare at the pathetic excuse of a man before me, my chest heaving with every breath I take. Without saying a single word, I raise the bat over my head. I maintain eye contact with Devan as I use every ounce of strength I have in me to smash out the windshield of his car. The coward doesn't so much as move as he gapes on in shock at the destruction I've caused. The driveway is littered with bits of plastic, metal, and shards of glass. Suddenly, the anger I felt moments ago dissipates, and calmness moves in. Pushing my hair out of my face, I smile. "Good to see ya, Devan." With that, I turn and walk back up the drive, leaving my ex with his mouth hanging open. Blake, who is sitting relaxed on his bike and smoking a cigarette, grins as I approach. When I'm within reach, he grips the back of my neck and kisses me. "Feel better?" He takes the bat from me, and I climb on behind him. Blake had his closure the day he watched his uncle take his final breath, laying all his demons to rest once and for all. Now, he gave me mine.

"Much better." I climb on behind him. "Let's go home."

Blake twists the throttle of his bike, and the engine roars to life. "You got it, baby."

CRYSTAL DANIELS
Two Pens
One Story
SANDY ALVAREZ